BEST LESBIAN ROMANCE 2012

BEST LESBIAN
ROMANCE
2012

EDITED BY
RADCLYFFE

CLEiS
PRESS

Published in the United States by Cleis Press, Inc., 2246 Sixth Street, Berkeley, California 94710.

Printed in the United States.
Cover design: Scott Idleman
Cover photograph: Getty Images
Text design: Frank Wiedemann
First Edition.
10 9 8 7 6 5 4 3 2 1

Trade paper ISBN: 978-1-57344-757-7
E-book ISBN: 978-1-57344-769-0

"Blazing June" © JL Merrow appeared in *Lesbian Cops: Erotic Investigations*, Cleis Press, 2011; "Clean Slate" © Lisabet Sarai appeared in *Smooth*, Cleis Press, 2010.

Contents

INTRODUCTION

Romance is a lot like art—the interpretation often exists in the eye of the beholder and may change with time, custom, or circumstance. Romance also defies discrete classification: it is at once an emotion, a language, a poetry cadence, a fiction genre, a film type, a narrative form. Romantic *love* has been called abiding, intimate, intense, idealistic, infinite, soulful, and consuming. All in all, the concept of romance as it applies to our most personal relationships is diverse, wide-ranging, and downright impossible to define. But we know it when we feel it—and that visceral pleasure is what these stories capture.

From the joy and awe of falling in love in Sheree L. Greer's "A Prom Story in Three Parts":

"The pleasure that I had always kept hidden, a tiny contentment, an eternal secret tucked deep inside myself, grew into something bigger, louder, and more powerful than I thought possible. It rushed over me in great oceanic waves, lifting me up, higher and higher and higher, carrying me away into the seductive expanse of the mysterious, the magical, and the unknown."

to rediscovering not just love, but self, in Lisabet Sarai's "Clean Slate":

"Don't you think you deserve some happiness?"
Did I? The notion was bewildering and exciting.
"I'll walk you out. Think about it, chica. What do you really want?"
She kissed me, long and hard, before she opened the door, and I thought that I knew."

to the soul-deep fulfillment of living with love in Evan Mora's "A Love Story":

"'Tell me a story.'
...It's all a story, isn't it? All these hours and days, the big and the small, the changing of seasons. All these months, all these years. Her head on my lap, our fingers entwined, dappled sunlight filtering down through the canopy we're under, a solid trunk older than us all at my back."

...within these pages are the reflections of our dreams, the memories of our precious moments, and the unique wonder of our special love stories.

Radclyffe, 2012

VANILLA, SUGAR, BUTTER, SALT

Anna Meadows

The girl inside the bakery waves every time Blake passes. Four times a day. Once on the way to work; twice for the walk to and from the park on her lunch break, even in the rain; once on the way home.

Blake isn't sure why. She's never been inside. But four times a day, she catches that smile, small but bright, and a slight tilt of the girl's head, just enough to ripple her hair. Blake has never been able to manage more than a single nod back, hands in her pockets.

The front of the bakery is mostly glass, so Blake has a few seconds to watch her on the way by. A few seconds, four times a day. A minute or two a week.

Every day the girl wears jeans or corduroys. Under the bakery's blue apron, she wears blouses the color of peonies or butter. Her bangs are long enough to brush her eyelids, making her squint when she's at the register. Her hair grazes her shoulders like a fall of molasses.

She's small, but her little bit of extra weight keeps her from looking fragile. It's not visible when she dresses for fall or winter. But whenever she reaches for a high shelf, exposing a band of her midriff, Blake catches that hint of softness that calls to mind yellow-gold cake and mocha frosting. Her arms and shoulders are almost wiry from the mixing she does by hand, because some recipes need the warmth of fingers.

Today the girl is not behind the glass. She's in front of the shop, watering the marigolds in the window boxes. She cups a hand over each one, yellow and orange, laughing lightly as the frills ripple against her palm.

"Would you like a free sample?" she asks when she sees Blake. "Red velvet."

Blake politely shakes her head. She does not like sweets, and not eating the little square of cake seems ruder than not taking it at all. She prefers salt. On her kitchen counter sits a jar of *fleur de sel*, the French sea salt her mother gave her last Christmas. In the pocket of her jeans, she carries a little tin of kosher salt. Everything needs it. Even the steak fries at her favorite diner. Right out of the kitchen, they're bland, but with a quarter teaspoon more salt and some malt vinegar, they're her favorite food.

Blake asks what kind of marigolds she's growing.

"Two kinds," she says, tipping the watering can. "Man-in-the-moon and common." She takes Blake's hand so suddenly that Blake stumbles. She spreads Blake's palm and fingers over a marigold head the size of an apple. Blake shudders at the feeling of the ruffled petals. She almost laughs.

Two days later, Blake drives home from the hardware store; a broken door frame needed wood screws. A woman on her way to meet a friend for coffee runs a red while putting on mascara in her side mirror, hitting Blake's passenger side. Blake's car skids like a pinecone on a frozen lake and comes to rest against an electrical box bordered by cranesbill geraniums. Blake does not wake up for the next four days. Her mother reads to her from a book of Welsh fairy tales that hasn't left the shelf since Blake was eleven. Her older brother reads to her from the newspaper, pointing out comma splices and dangling modifiers along the way. Her father spends little time in her room. He checks up with the doctors and makes twice-daily calls to the insurance company. The owner of the bookshop where Blake works dabs a handkerchief at the corners of her eyes while telling Blake she must get better and come back, because her temporary replacement thinks *The Diary of Samuel Pepys* belongs in the fiction section. An old college roommate shows up with a girlfriend, a vase of yellow-eyed daisies, and two Mylar balloons.

When she wakes, her brother is slumped in a chair with the business section, after falling asleep mid-article. He hears her weak groans, stirs, and runs out into the hall so quickly he startles an orderly.

Her mother cries when Blake remembers her own name. Her father tells her the accident paperwork is all taken care of, and if she can sign here and initial here, the insurance company will take care of getting her another car. Her cousins bring her a patty melt and steak fries from her favorite diner, along with the little tin of kosher salt and a plastic container of malt vinegar. She thanks them, eats half the sandwich, and does not touch the steak fries.

She doesn't use the salt. She doesn't want it.

The next time Blake passes the bakery, her first day back at work, the girl in the window waves. She doesn't stare at the sling where Blake's arm hangs or at the faint scarring near her hairline. She offers Blake the same smile and comes out to the sidewalk with a ceramic plate, robin's-egg blue and full of cake squares.

"Would you like a free sample?" She offers Blake vanilla beneath a cloud-cover of lemon frosting.

Blake takes it and thanks her.

"You like it?" the girl asks.

Blake says yes.

"Really," the girl says. "Be honest. It's a new recipe."

Blake tells her it's perfect. She asks for one of the same, lemon on vanilla.

The girl nestles two in a small box, robin's-egg blue. "On me," she says when Blake tries to pay. "First-time customer."

Blake protests, but the girl holds up a hand to stop her. Her fingernails are short, but manicured and polished shell pink.

"You'll be back," she says.

That night, after fixing the door frame that went unrepaired the day she bought the wood screws, Blake eats one of the cupcakes along with the dose of painkillers that lets her sleep. The frosting, petal soft, reminds her of lemon blossoms. The cake spreads butter and honey and vanilla sugar over her tongue. She eats the second for breakfast the next morning, after her over-easy egg and tomato on sourdough. No salt this time—the grains of vanilla sugar fit into the little space the salt used to fill.

She stops by the bakery on her way home from work the next day. The girl is making roses out of pink and yellow marzipan. She rolls tiny pieces of almond paste into balls and presses them into petals with the pad of her thumb.

"What can I get for you today?" the girl asks, finishing the outer petals.

Blake asks what she recommends.

"Mexican mocha," the girl says. "If you like cinnamon. It's my grandmother's recipe."

Blake says she likes cinnamon.

The girl boxes one up. "There's a little bit of chili powder, but you won't taste it. It just brings out everything else."

Blake hands her a credit card and ID.

The girl checks the ID. "Blake," she says. "I like it." She hands them back along with the box.

Blake looks for a name tag, but the girl isn't wearing one. So she says thank you and slides the cards into her back pocket, next to her medical insurance card, which she's gotten in the habit of carrying.

"Wait," the girl says. She opens the box, sets a marzipan rose on top of the frosting, and closes the lid. "There."

She takes Blake's good hand and shakes it, her grip firmer than her small fingers suggest. "I'm Aimee."

Aimee. Blake has thought of her as the girl from the bakery for more than a year, but the open vowels of her name fit her so well, it's an easy replacement.

That night, Blake slowly peels the paper wrapper from the cupcake. She eats it slowly, letting the dark cocoa and coffee bloom against the bite of the chili powder and cinnamon. She eats the rose last, closing her eyes and trying to make out the contours of Aimee's thumbprint on each petal.

Blake comes in every day, sometimes on her way home from work, sometimes on her lunch-hour walk. She needs sugar, once daily, like a vitamin. Each time, Blake hands over her ID along with her credit card, as though Aimee doesn't know her name and face. Each time she asks Aimee what she recommends. Some days it's coconut, the top covered in flakes like a quarter-inch of new snow. Others it's the wine-colored cherries of Black Forest, the warm spice of caramel pear with clover honey, or chocolate mint, the dark cocoa powder only giving up the burst of pepper-mint at the last moment. On Fridays, Aimee often suggests the strawberry lemonade, because it's the only day they make it. The frosting is blush pink, dotted with fuchsia sprinkles. Blake would never eat something that looked so much like a sofa pillow if Aimee didn't pick it.

A few Fridays later, the first after Blake's doctor says she can stop wearing her sling, Aimee seems distracted. Her shoulders are tense, and she taps her nails whenever she rests a hand on the counter.

Blake hands Aimee her ID and credit card and asks for whatever she recommends today.

"Anything," Aimee says. "They're all good." She barely looks at Blake. She doesn't smile at her or the two other customers browsing the counter.

Blake waits, studying the Formica floor. When Aimee says nothing else, she mumbles that she'll come back later and wanders out onto the sidewalk. She closes up the bookshop and goes home. She lies on the sofa, staring up at the popcorn ceiling while her hunger for sugar wears on her.

She's almost asleep when a few muted knocks wake her. She gets to her feet, shaking out the left side of her body on her way to the door. Since the accident, that side falls asleep more easily than her right.

Aimee stands in the hall. An oversized purse, the canvas printed with tea roses, hangs from her shoulder. It's so big, and there's so much fabric, it makes her look even shorter.

Blake wonders how she knows where she lives until she takes her credit card and ID from an inner pocket.

"You left these." She tips the cards, looking at the ID. "Today's your birthday." She hands it to Blake. "Why aren't you with your family?"

Blake says they don't live around here, that she'll see them over the weekend.

Aimee takes one of the bakery's blue boxes from her purse. "I brought you a maple and a plain chocolate." She hands it to Blake. "I didn't know what you'd be in the mood for."

Blake says thank you, not knowing if it'd be more polite to invite her in or let her get home.

"I'm sorry about earlier," Aimee says. "I was having a hard time."

Blake doesn't ask, and hopes it doesn't have something to do with a boyfriend. If Aimee wants to say more, she will.

Aimee goes up and down on the balls of her feet, deepening the crease in the sky blue canvas of her lo-tops. "I was testing a new recipe. I usually get it on the first couple of tries. My boss says I have the magic touch."

She comes in without Blake asking her. Blake likes that, not just because it saves her from asking, but also because she's the kind of girl who doesn't need to be asked. Few people would guess that from her pastel blouses and strawberry-colored lipstick.

"But I've been trying one all week and I can't get it," Aimee says.

Blake asks what she thinks is wrong with it. Aimee pulls another box from her purse and sets it on the kitchen counter. "You tell me. I took the extras home to try and figure out what I did wrong."

Blake carefully lifts the lid—vanilla cake with frosting the color of antique gold roses, capped with round sugar beads, tiny and cream-colored.

"Try it," Aimee says. "Tell me what's wrong. I can take it."

Blake pulls off a small piece and lets it dissolve on her tongue. She cocks her head, considering. The caramel flavor is soft and even, but it lacks the spice she's come to love in Aimee's baking.

"It's bland, isn't it?" asks Aimee.

Blake tells her it's still better than almost any cupcake she's ever had.

"It's bland," Aimee says.

Blake cocks her head to the other side and admits it's not as good as the ones Aimee usually makes.

Aimee takes a bite off the same one Blake tried. She stares into space as she swallows. "It needs something."

Blake tries it again, her mouth overlapping the shape of Aimee's bite. She tells her it needs salt.

"Salt?" Aimee asks.

Blake says yes.

"There's already salt in there," Aimee says.

Blake asks what kind of salt.

"What do you mean what kind of salt?" Aimee asks. "Table salt."

Blake shakes her head and finds the jar of *fleur de sel* her mother gave her. She lifts the lid and tilts the jar to the light, showing Aimee how the grains sparkle like snowflakes. She says Aimee should use this. Aimee looks skeptical. Blake says she should trust her. Aimee says she'll be right back.

Twelve minutes later she returns with a grocery bag from the corner store. She spreads its contents out on Blake's counter. Flour, white sugar, molasses sugar. Butter, brown eggs, cream, pure vanilla.

She mixes the cake batter with a wooden spoon while Blake finds a muffin pan her mother gave her when she got her first apartment. With a nod from Aimee, Blake adds to the batter as much *fleur de sel* as she can pinch between her thumb and two fingers.

Once the cake is in the oven, Aimee heats sugar and a little water in a saucepan until it turns deep amber. She stirs in heavy cream and vanilla, while Blake adds a sprinkle of *fleur de sel* that wafts down to the caramel like the petals of spring blossoms. When it cools enough to touch, Aimee spreads a thimbleful onto her finger and offers it to Blake, who tries not to blush as she licks it off the polished pink of Aimee's nail. The caramel tastes rounder and fuller, like a peony that's opened without warning. "Better?" Aimee asks, and Blake nods. Aimee smiles and produces a KitchenAid mixer from her bag.

Blake asks why she carries a hand mixer in her purse.

"It's my baby," Aimee says, and kisses the pastel pink enamel. "I'm not leaving it there overnight."

Blake can't help smiling. She used to carry kosher salt in her pocket, so who was she to judge. She removes the cake from the oven while Aimee blends the caramel with butter and a little more *fleur de sel*.

Aimee spreads frosting onto a still-warm cupcake and drags her forefinger through. Her candy-colored tongue laps it away from her fingertip. Her eyes fall shut. She swallows. Her eyes open, and she wraps her arms around Blake's shoulders and kisses her, the taste of vanilla and salted caramel still on her lips.

"It's perfect," Aimee says.

Blake smiles, holding her breath to keep her balance.

"Here." Aimee pulls off a piece of the cake, sliding extra frosting on, and brings it to Blake's mouth. Blake hesitates. Even though Aimee just kissed her, she's shy about her lips brushing Aimee's fingers again. But Aimee brings the piece close enough that the frosting grazes her mouth. She accepts it, and the flavor of dark vanilla warms her tongue. She can't taste the *fleur de sel*, but it makes the caramelized sugar glow.

Blake tells her she's right. It's perfect.

Aimee nods, almost giggling, and kisses her again. Blake catches the cherry vanilla of her lip gloss; her tongue feels like wet brown sugar. Aimee presses her body into Blake's. She's soft. She gives her weight to Blake's right side, like she knows the left is still sore even though the sling is gone.

Blake unties the bakery apron Aimee is still wearing and pulls off her blouse. Aimee unbuttons Blake's shirt, leaving her undershirt because she can feel her breasts through the thin cotton. Their fingers tangle as they unbutton each other's jeans. Aimee finds brushed cotton under Blake's fly; Blake finds lace that dampens under her touch.

Aimee spreads a patch of frosting onto Blake's collarbone when she has her eyes closed. She licks it away and kisses Blake when it's only half-melted on her lips. Blake frees Aimee's left breast from her bra and spreads caramel over the circle of pink at the tip. Aimee throws her head back as Blake kisses her a dozen times to clear it, her hand pulling aside the lace of her panties and finding the softness underneath, like the frilled petals of marigolds.

By the time the muffin pan cools to room temperature, their clothes cover the floor of the apartment kitchen. The scent of salt and caramel still hovers like sugar clouds. Aimee's fingers play at Blake's underwear, drawing out her wetness until she aches and throbs for direct touch and her longing soaks a patch of the heavy cotton. Aimee lifts the waistband and eases her fingers inside so slowly that Blake startles when Aimee finds her little point of hardness, like a round bead of carnelian. When she finishes, she barely takes a breath before she turns Aimee onto her back and kisses the inside of each of her thighs, alternating, drawing closer to the center each time. Aimee moves her hips with impatience, but she laughs with the pleasure of waiting. When Blake reaches the midpoint between her thighs, she finds the sugar and salt of her, like *fleur de sel* and wildflower honey.

TRAINING OP

Radclyffe

I'm a federal agent, not a soldier, so "don't ask, don't tell" doesn't apply. That's a good thing for me, since pretending I'm someone I'm not just doesn't fly. Oh, I can hide what I'm feeling all right. When I'm working my guy, standing post at the edge of a crowd, observing, assessing, I have the perfect Secret Agent poker face. For some reason, people always try to get me to laugh or engage in conversation, as if the very fact that I'm there to protect someone isn't really all that important. A few seconds of stony silence usually convinces them to move along.

But in the off hours when it's just us agents—waiting, checking the weapons, preparing the vehicles—conversation predictably flows from sports to movies to good-natured gossip. And gossip always leads to sex. At least talking about it. The guys don't care I'm a lesbian, and they're too polite or too shy or just too nice to ask for details. It's my straight *female* fellow agents who are the real problems. They like to flirt just to see if their suggestive comments can make me blush, and when I finally do, they tease me all the more. They're my friends, they have my back, they know me better than my family, and I don't mind the flirting. It passes the time. Except for Kris. I've been more than nine-tenths of the way in love with her for years, and when she flirts, it hits me hard and stays with me. All the way back to my lonely room and my empty bed, where I think of her sometimes—okay, a lot of times—when I come.

Kris and I were in the same recruiting class and shared a room for the whole training period. She had a boyfriend at the time, another agent. Liaisons between agents are pretty common because when you work fourteen hours at a stretch and your schedule changes from one day to the next and you're doing things you can't always talk about, it's tough to maintain a relationship with someone outside the agency. I was single then and still am. I don't have a lot of time to date, and honestly, there just aren't that many women I meet off the job who turn me on. And the ones who do all remind me of Kris, and somehow, that kind of kills the mood.

After training, Kris got posted to the New York field office and I ended up on a permanent personal protection detail. Fortunately, I wasn't that far away and whenever our schedules meshed, we'd grab lunch or dinner. She was really the only one from the original class of recruits I kept up with. So when we discovered we'd both be attending the Women in Federal Law Enforcement meeting, we immediately made plans to share a room.

Arriving at the hotel that first afternoon, I felt the same spurt of excitement I had the first day I showed up for training ops. Kris dumped her luggage on the floor by her bed and grinned at me across the hotel room. "Just like old times."

"Yeah, except we're not green recruits anymore…" We finished together with our insiders' mantra: "We're Big Bad Federal Agents!"

Kris cracked up and flopped on her back onto one of the queen-sized beds. We were about the same age (early thirties) and the same height and weight (average and average), but the similarity ended there. She loved to box and her shoulders were broad, her thighs muscular, and her ass strong and hard. I was a runner, lankier and leaner. With shoulder-length hair so black it looked blue in the sunlight and dark chocolate eyes, she was the exact opposite of my strawberry-blond, blue-eyed coloring. I even had a few freckles scattered over my nose that got more prominent in the summer. And of course, when I blushed I couldn't hide it.

I fell onto the other bed and rolled onto my side, staring at her across the divide. She was every bit as beautiful and sexy as I remembered, and I got the old familiar ache deep down inside I always got when I looked at her. We'd shared so much. Not just the physical and mental rigors of training, but in the dark, late at night, we'd shared our uncertainties and even our fears. Somewhere in those quiet hours, I'd fallen in love with her.

"So did you start dating that guy Rodney you told me was interested?" I asked to remind myself not to go down that road again.

"Nope." Kris reached over her head to grab a pillow and curled up to face me with it against her chest, her arms wrapped around it like a lover. "Haven't been dating anyone recently."

"Too busy?"

"Not that so much," she said, her eyes seeming to be searching mine. "I just felt like I was going through the motions, you know?"

"Uh, isn't that the point?" I started to make a suggestive hand motion and she threw the pillow at me.

"I forgot what a pig you are."

"Me?" I sat up on the side of the bed, feigning innocence.

"Who was it that leaned over in class one afternoon and whispered, 'You've got really great breasts. If I were into girls, I'd be all over them'?"

Kris laughed. "Come on. How many times did we hear the same talk about probable cause and right to search? Your breasts were way more interesting!"

"And I'm just saying you're *way* more bad than me."

"So how about you," Kris asked while staring at me hard. "Got a steady girlfriend yet?"

"Who has time?" I got up quickly, wanting to change the subject. Talking about why I wasn't with anyone, especially with the woman I really wanted to be with, just plain hurt. "Come on. Let's go downstairs to the bar and see if anyone else we know has shown up."

The lobby was jammed with women, most wearing shirts with law enforcement logos, and a few random men who looked like their eyes were about to fall out of their heads. Not every woman was beautiful, at least not in the conventional sense, but every single one was confident and capable, and there's nothing quite as sexy as a woman who knows she can handle anything. We finally elbowed our way into the bar and snagged the last stool.

"Go ahead," I said to Kris. "You take it. I had a long flight and I'm tired of sitting."

We finally got our drinks and were swapping work stories when a guy in a rumpled business suit wedged himself partway between me and the stool where Kris was sitting. His eyes were bloodshot, his expression slack, and his breath a hundred proof.

Looking at me, he slurred, "Hi, gorgeous. I could use some company and you fit the bill."

"Thanks, but I'm not interested," I said while trying to get enough room in the cramped space to divert any physical move he might make in my direction.

"We could have fun," he said, swaying toward me.

"She said she's not interested," Kris said with a bite to her voice I'd never heard before.

"It's okay," I said quietly. The guy was drunk but he wasn't dangerous. He'd get bored in a second and wander off.

"No, it isn't."

I'd never heard Kris sound so serious or seen her look quite so fierce. She was so wired she was vibrating, and I wanted to run my hand down her arm just to soothe her. Of course I didn't. I tried never to touch her casually, because even the slightest contact was never casual for me.

"Listen, honey," the guy started to say, but he never had a chance to finish.

Kris grabbed a fistful of my polo shirt, right between my breasts, and yanked me toward her. "She's with me."

And the next thing I knew, she was kissing me. On the mouth. And she wasn't holding back. I was so stunned, I didn't resist when her tongue skated over my lower lip. I opened my mouth and breathed her in like I'd been underwater for hours and finally surfaced. She made a tiny sound in the back of her throat that only I could hear. A little moan of pleasure. My stomach turned a somersault, and I was instantly wet.

When she finally let me go, I was panting as if I'd just finished running an obstacle course. Sometime during the kiss she'd opened her legs and I'd stepped between them, and now she held me between her thighs, my pelvis snugged up against hers. I was afraid she'd feel my clitoris pounding right through my jeans.

"Nice move, Kris." I was trying to act like we kissed every day, but my voice sounded rusty and unused and I was shaking all over. I think the guy left then. I'm not sure. It didn't matter.

All that mattered was the look in her eyes. A little hazy and a little hot.

"I think we should go upstairs," Kris said.

"It *is* kind of noisy and crowded down here."

"Uh-huh." Kris stood up and her whole body slid against mine.

I whimpered at the all-over tingle and she laughed. Then she took my hand and said, "Come on."

She pulled me through the crowd and I followed witlessly. What the hell had just happened? She didn't really mean that kiss, did she? Oh God, what if she didn't? What if she *did*?

By some miracle the elevator was nearly empty, and we staked out the back corner for the ride up to the twentieth floor. I leaned against the wall because my legs were shaking so bad I was afraid I would slide down to the floor. We stopped on five and a group of women with matching alphabet agency polos got on and Kris backed up. Right into me. Her ass settled firmly into my crotch and when we started up, she tightened her butt and I felt as if she was squeezing me right through my jeans.

I groaned and closed my eyes. Maybe she didn't know what she was doing to me. I lightly clasped her hips and she didn't move away. Maybe she did know.

"We're here," Kris whispered and I realized the elevator had stopped and a redhead with a big smile was holding the door open for us. "Let's go, BBFA."

Somehow I managed to get down the hall on rubbery legs and Kris keyed us into our suite. We'd left the desk lamp on and the beds loomed large in the dimly lit room. I halted just inside the door and Kris turned back, reached around me, and flipped the security bar on the lock. Her breasts brushed mine.

"Kris?" I asked.

She merely smiled, took both my hands, and pulled me

toward the bed. When we reached it, she said, "You first."

I was trying to read her face, find the message in her eyes. What were we doing? What did she want? I knew what I wanted. What I'd always wanted. Her.

When I didn't move quickly enough, she pressed her fingertips against my shoulders and pushed me backward. I went with the motion and ended up on my back, half sitting up against the pillows. She followed and straddled me, leaning over with her arms braced beside my shoulders, her body almost but not quite touching mine.

"Are you sure you want to do this?" I asked.

"Very sure," she said.

That mouth of hers, the one I was so used to seeing smirking at me over some private joke, smiling during the rough times when only laughter could still the tears, that mouth with the full perfectly curved lips, wide and generous, came down over mine with gentle certainty. God, she could kiss. She ran the tip of her tongue over the surface of my lower lip, as if tasting a brand-new flavor, slowly, thoroughly, savoring. Propped up against the back of the bed, my hands open helplessly at my sides, I sat perfectly still and let her discover whatever it was she was seeking. She kept her eyes open when she kissed, which didn't surprise me at all. She was that kind of girl. Direct, bold, adventurous. And honest. She didn't hide what she was feeling, it was there in her eyes as her rich chocolaty irises grew hazy and her wide dark pupils expanded. When her tongue dipped into my mouth, soft and warm, her lids lowered lazily then opened again, as if she'd just found some secret pleasure. I sucked lightly, pulling her tongue deeper, and she whimpered once, a high-pitched, sweet cry of surprise. Her breasts brushed mine and her nipples peaked beneath the thin cotton shirt that matched mine.

When she pulled away I followed, my lips still hungrily parted, but she stopped me with her palm pressed firmly in the center of my chest.

"Take your pants off."

"If I do," I said, my voice tight and raspy, "I won't be responsible for—"

"You're right. I'm responsible."

She swept her hand slowly back and forth over my chest, letting her fingers stray over my nipples. They were hard and tight and aching. I groaned.

"Everything. Off. Now."

I watched her face while I unbuttoned my pants, slipped the zipper down. The corners of her mouth curved upward, her eyes danced. She was enjoying my helplessness. Her fingers closed on my nipple, squeezed, and my back arched.

"Your hands are shaking," she said casually.

"I can't help it. I've wanted you for so long."

Her face changed, became at once fierce and soft. She released my breast and shifted beside me. While I fumbled with my pants, she leaned on one elbow and worked her hand beneath my polo shirt, rubbing my stomach in small circles with her fingertips. I watched her hand move under my shirt, my clitoris so tight I hurt to move. Lifting my hips, I stripped everything down and kicked my shoes and clothes off the bottom of the bed.

"Your stomach is so hard," she whispered, running her nails up and down the center of my belly. "Are you excited, sweetie?"

"Guns are hot." I laughed, sounding desperate to my own ears. My naked legs were board-stiff, flexed so tight they barely touched the bed. I stared at her wandering fingers moving lower, barely grazing the trimmed patch at the apex of my thighs. I couldn't seem to take a full breath, anticipating her touch, fearing she would stop. *Control, control, control,* I told myself, terrified I would pop the second she touched me.

She pressed three fingertips against the base of my clitoris and stopped. Just stopped. I throbbed beneath her, so fast and so hard I felt like I was buzzing.

"Wow." She looked at me with an expression of innocent wonder. "Is that for me?"

"Can't you tell?" Just the sight of her touching me, the reality so much more exquisite than the fantasy, was enough to make me come. I felt a warning pulse deep inside and my head jerked back against the headboard. "Oh God, don't move for a second."

"Why, what's happening? Are you close already?" She sounded breathless. Her face was right next to mine, her eyes swirling with dark shadows.

"Right on the edge."

"I don't want you to come right away." She kissed me, one fast hard thrust of her tongue, and the heat of her mouth shot straight between my legs. She grinned when I gasped. "Don't come yet, okay?"

"Just stay still, then. Let me get a grip."

She laughed and kissed me and didn't stop this time. She tasted so good. Her tongue stroked mine and my clit pumped hard against her fingers. I grabbed her wrist and yanked her hand away. She strained to break my hold on her arm, and we wrestled while she plunged her tongue deeper into my mouth. I bit her tongue just short of hard and she made a little growl and rolled on top of me. Her thigh settled between mine, and she thrust and rocked her pelvis while we thrashed around the bed, kissing and grappling for dominance.

She finally pinned me and said in her command voice, "Give it up. I want to see you. All of you."

I relented. I'd give her anything she wanted. I pulled my polo shirt and tank top off over my head and threw them somewhere into the room. Then I fell back against the pillows and opened my legs. "Go ahead."

She glanced down, then met my eyes, hers sparkling. "Yeah? Can I touch now too?"

I really tried to hold on to my cool, but my eyes did a slow roll back into my head. She laughed, sounding really proud of herself, and kissed my stomach as she slid a little ways down on the bed.

"Is that a yes?" she asked.

"Yes. Please." I sounded like I was begging. I *was* begging.

"This is so much fun," she whispered and shoved all the way down between my legs. Then she paused and looked up at me, her playful smile growing tender. "Are you okay, sweetie?"

"Perfect. I want to watch you make me come."

"Oh yeah." She parted me ever so gently with her fingertips, and my clit sprang up, thick and dark and wet. Her eyes widened. "God. Did I really do that to you?"

"The second you kissed me."

She made a little humming sound of pleasure and kissed it, just a quick light brush of her lips. I jerked, and the humming sound she made turned into a growl. Ever so slowly she puckered her moist lips and sealed them around me, slowly drawing her mouth up and off.

"Look at that," she whispered. "I can see it jumping."

"I'm really close to coming."

"No freaking kidding. I can't believe how hard you are." She laughed shakily and pressed her fingertip against the base, making it jut out. Then she licked it.

"If you do that again, I'm going to come right in your mouth."

"I want you to." She massaged me with her fingertip and watched my face. "It's nice of you to warn me, though, so we don't finish too fast."

I banged my head against the wall. "Kris, damn it. I really have to come."

"It's my first time." She kissed the spot she'd been stroking with her fingertip. "I don't want to miss anything."

"It just feels so good." I was whining, couldn't help it. "You make me want to come so bad."

Her eyes got all dark and dangerous again. "Do I?"

"All the time."

"Really now." She dropped her head, sucking me in. The instant she tongued me, I started to come. She pulled back in surprise and my shoulders jerked off the pillows.

"Don't you fucking stop!"

She sucked me again and my body did a wild dance. My legs twisted, my stomach hollowed, and I shouted prayers and profanity while I came all over her mouth.

Eventually I lay boneless and quivering, but she never stopped licking and fondling me. Tears ran from my eyes and my fingers twitched in the sheets. She'd pretty much destroyed me. When she started rubbing her cheek over my wet, throbbing pussy, I moaned.

"Too much?" she asked.

"Too good," I gasped.

Just as quickly as she'd started, she rolled away. "Oh God, I have to get out of these clothes."

She ripped off her shirt and pants, flinging things everywhere. Then she was naked, gloriously naked. I'd seen her naked dozens of times before, but never like this. Her upthrust breasts were tight, the pink nipples puckered. Her chest and neck were flushed a rich rose. Her face held a question, the first time I'd seen her look uncertain since we'd walked into the room.

"God, you're beautiful." I opened my arms. "Get down here."

She threw herself on me, catching herself on her outstretched arms as her hips landed between mine. I clasped both calves around the backs of her thighs, rubbing my clit over hers. She panted, staring into my eyes, grinding into me.

"I've been thinking about this for a long, long time." She worried her lower lip between her teeth, frown lines cutting between her brows. "You feel so good. I'm so turned on."

I cradled her breasts and squeezed. She rode me harder.

"Can you come this way?" she gasped.

"Yes."

She threw her head back, her lips parting in surprise. "Oh shit. I think I'm going to come. Oh damn it." Her muscular arms trembled beside my shoulders and she dropped her head to catch my gaze. "I don't want to, but I don't think I can stop."

"Don't try." I pumped her nipples. "Come if you want to." I pushed a hand between us, opened myself, then pulled her tight into me with my legs around her waist. "Come on me."

She rolled her clit over mine, a broken chain of cries escaping from her throat. I kneaded her clenched ass. She worked herself around and around on my already too-sensitive clit. That's when I heard myself mumbling and knew I was losing it.

"You're making me come again," I groaned.

"Oh me too. Oh God, right now." She threw back her head and whined, jerking hard between my legs. My clit spasmed and I came right after her.

When she collapsed with a gut-deep moan, I wrapped my arms around her and cradled her face in the curve of my neck. I didn't know what came next and was afraid to ask. After a while, she kissed my throat and burrowed closer. I pulled the sheet over us.

"Are you okay?" Kris asked.

"Great."

"Surprised?"

I laughed. "Totally blown away."

She feathered her fingers over my nipple and I twitched.

"Are you always this sexy?" she asked.

"Only with you." I meant it and I hoped she knew.

"I almost kissed you outside the restaurant the last time we had dinner." Kris rubbed her cheek over my breast. "And about a dozen times before that. I couldn't wait any longer."

"Kris, what—"

"Before you say anything else," Kris whispered, "you should know I've fallen in love with you. I don't know why it took me so long to figure that out."

"You always were a slow study." She bit my shoulder and I just hugged her closer. "I love you too. Have for years."

"You didn't think to tell me?"

"I didn't think there was any chance."

Kris pushed up and gave me a look that said I was an idiot. "Now who's the slow study?"

"Maybe with a little more training I'll get it right."

"Maybe we should find out," she said. And then she kissed me.

FRENCH FRIED

Rachel Kramer Bussel

As I'm walking down the Rue de Rivoli, I see something through the window of an otherwise unassuming restaurant that makes me stop in my tracks. Sitting there, looking impossibly chic, eating long, skinny fries with a fork as a fire burns beneath the plate, keeping them perpetually warm, is a woman, stunningly beautiful even for Paris, and that's saying something. She looks impish, delicate and sexy, yet also strong, as she blows gently on the fries, looking like she owns the restaurant, if not the entire city. There are a few other customers, but no one seated near her, so I have a perfect view. She eats one or two at a time, letting them pass between her beautifully glossed red lips, her black hair gleaming straight down her back. There's no other food on the table, just a glass of water and a hardcover book opened to the middle. Her nails are as red and shiny as her lips, and she shuts her eyes as she takes each bite, to fully savor it, then opens them when she reaches for another fry.

I check my own reflection in the window. Typical tourist is

what I figure, though I've added an extra layer of mascara and new purple eyeliner, and my normally boring brunette hair is freshly highlighted, my last errand before leaving home. My jeans are dark and tight, accenting my ass, something French women don't have in quite the abundance we Americans do. I'm a size ten, curvy and healthy, but at five foot three, short—nothing like the tall human gazelles I've seen plenty of in just one day.

Most of these Parisian women I've encountered intimidate me, but this one intrigues me immediately. I'm sure I'm blushing, and if I haven't been before, I must be when she catches me looking and winks, and even though I barely speak any French, I smile back. I've come here on a whim, to get away from the girls back home in New York, the ones who all seem to know each other, where it's almost impossible to make a fresh start. Sometimes I like the small-worldness of my local dyke scene, where within a few questions you can pinpoint how your ex and her ex were college roommates or something, but it can be stifling, and I just want some fun, no drama. I had extra vacation time I needed to use or lose, and the way my friends who love Paris talked about it made me choose it over some beach resort. I like cities, with all their hustle and bustle and anonymity, but my own has felt much too cloying for comfort. This one, though, is brand-new, wide open, as if waiting just for me.

I think the same of the girl I'm staring at as I keep watching. The French fry girl looks like just the antidote to my problems, and when she crooks one beautiful finger and beckons me inside, I race in from the cold, feeling my nipples harden even once I'm inside the warmth of the restaurant.

"Hello," she says, the two syllables beautifully accented, to my ears sounding almost like a foreign, sensual language. She smiles apologetically before spearing another fry, popping it into her mouth, chewing, swallowing, and saying, "I'm Véronique."

I have to snap out of staring mode and remind myself she isn't the star of some sexy, exotic movie, but a real, live, gorgeous woman, one who is talking to me! I hadn't expected to make any new friends on this trip, but rather, the opposite; to be lost and alone and wandering, to avoid all the madness back home that made me feel like I could barely walk down the street, to escape.

But I've never had a random woman hit on me like that, out of the blue, not at a club, in the middle of the day, and certainly not one as striking as she is. "Hi," I say, my voice quiet. "I'm Anna."

"Sit, *s'il vous plait*. Share?" Her English is halting, but lovely, the words striking tones you just don't hear in the States. I nod, staring at her, soaking her in, from the round arches of her eyebrows to the fine black pencil lining her brown eyes, the lashes lush, the cheeks rosy. She stares at me intently, and only breaks the stare to lift a fry with her fingers and hold it out to my lips. "Open," she says, and I do. I couldn't have done otherwise.

The fry is the best thing I've ever tasted. It's warm and perfectly cooked through, salty, with a hint of some kind of spice. But what heats my mouth even more is the way Véronique is looking at me. Her eyes are taking in my entire face, wide, trusting, seeking, and her lips are red and beautiful. On someone else the color might look overbearing, a vamp on the prowl, but on her it manages to look both innocent and seductive. I'm not afraid of her in the least, nor of her hungry eyes just waiting to devour me like I am doing to the fries. The fork lingers between her perfectly manicured fingers, but she puts it down, then picks up another fry and runs it along my lower lip. I dart out my tongue, teasing the fry, running my tongue up its length, licking the salt off.

She laughs, the sound melodious, but suddenly I want to

feed her too. I part my lips and she traces a fry along each one, from the right edge where they meet, along my lower lip, then around and atop the curves of my upper lip, getting the salty potato sticky with my gloss while her eyes soak in every inch of my face. Her look is intense, whether from under those impossibly long lashes or straight on. This is a look I never get from the New York girls, who like to keep their distance. I want to tell her I don't speak French, but when I open my mouth, she traces the fry along my tongue. The back of my throat catches. Even though we are flirting over skinny bits of fried potatoes, there's nothing innocent about this. I know little more than this woman's name and already I want all of her, inside and out.

She is so calm, I can only wonder if her heart is beating fast too. "More?" She inches closer to me, and all the thoughts about touching up my makeup, straightening my outfit, wondering what I'm doing leave my head as she slips me another fry, this time letting her finger dance along my tongue as she does. I press upward against the pad of her finger as she traces it against my organ, and know right away we are doing much more than eating. We are communicating in a language we are both perfectly fluent in, and the delicate hairs along my arms rise up in greeting.

She is so clearly in charge of me, and yet she's not dominating me. As her finger bends and the smooth edge of her nail scrapes my skin, I relax even more. She is teasing me, right here in this bistro, in a city I'd never stepped foot in until yesterday. She is daring me to stay silent, to not rush forward with the torrent of questions I find so tedious about dating back home. She is daring me to simply sit, wait, savor. She pulls out her finger and wipes it on her napkin, then picks up another fry, dips it in a pool of ketchup that somehow now seems like a sex sauce whipped up just for us, and puts it in her mouth.

I sense a couple walking in and look up, my cheeks flaming, like I've been caught doing something wrong. Véronique's laugh tickles the air. *I'm the only one who matters here*, her face seems to say to me. "Beautiful," she says softly. She is a woman of few words, and I sense that it's not because of the language barrier. In fact, though this feels like a dream, I don't feel the barriers I usually do when trying to talk to a girl I like, sober, *sans* pretenses. She alternates putting a fry in her mouth with putting one in mine, and even when I'm full, I keep eating, if only for the chance to taste her fingers against my lips. I move closer and closer to her until our sides are joined. I have a sudden urge to lean my head on her shoulder, but I stop myself; I don't truly know her, even though it feels like I do.

I have so many questions for her. They seem to bubble up from my insides, but for once I hold them back. This isn't about food, but it isn't about talking either. She leans over and nips at my earlobe and I practically come. Véronique is seducing me with every move she makes, even with the ones she doesn't make. When she turns her head to wave one dainty hand in the air for the check, the curve of her eyelashes consumes me. I see a tattoo peeking out from beneath her wall of shiny hair and want to kiss it, want to trace it, want to know all about why she got it.

Instead I just silently admire its edges, this hint of ink, and all too soon we are down to the last French fry. She gives me a look that is pure sex kitten, her perfect red lips pursed, eyebrows arched, as if daring me to take it. But then Véronique changes course. She takes my arm and lifts my palm to her lips, bending my hand just so, in order to bite the edge of my palm, to sink her teeth into it. This is not a nibble, like we've been doing with the fries, but a mark, a claim. She does it again and again and I am totally captivated. Who is she? How did she get so bold? Forget *French Women Don't Get Fat*—how about *French Women*

Don't Get Intimidated? She is every inch the conquering queen, and I, her subject.

"Kiss me," she murmurs, then lifts me up so I am straddling her, but somehow, in a way that isn't obscene. Must be another trick of the French, I figure, as our lips touch, our salty, warm mouths meeting. We could be over-the-top, could make a scene, but her tongue is gentle, tender, kind. Buried underneath her bombshell look is a true romantic, a sweet girl offering me her mouth as a peace offering, even though we aren't at war.

No sooner has she introduced her tongue to mine than Véronique pulls away and places me back in my seat. The waitress arrives with the check. From her sleek black clutch purse, Véronique removes some colorful bills and delicately places them next to the check. I have no idea if she is going to stand up and swoop out of the room, cast me aside, leave me burning just as the flame beneath her now-empty plate burns, blue and orange and full of desire.

She does stand up, and I admire her backside, the way the pearly white blouse meets the edge of her black skirt, smoothed along the curves of her ass, memorize it in case this is the last time I will ever see it. I won't mind, I vow to myself, to God, to whoever might be listening. Already my entire mind-set has changed; I am no longer just a tourist, just a lost girl wandering in a foreign city. I am part of its magic, and its magic has seeped into my skin as well.

Then Véronique turns and pierces me with her gaze, her blue eyes direct beneath those endless lashes. She's slipped on a pair of elegant white gloves in the few moments I've been taking in her behind, and she offers me a hand. I stand and take it, and we walk outside, leaving the flame burning on the table, off to quench our own flames, ones we don't need to speak aloud to stoke.

RULE 4

Cheyenne Blue

My new housemate was everything I was not.

"I'm going for a run," she'd say, bouncing on her toes, dressed in something clingy and brief, all tanned lithe limbs, muscle, and bone. I'd dip into a bag of Hershey's Kisses, searching for the ones I like best—the white chocolate ones—and settle myself more comfortably on the couch. "See you later. There'll be dinner when you return if you're interested."

"What are you cooking?" Joanna would bend to tie her shoelace tighter. Whether by accident or design, I could see up the leg of her shorts to the plain cotton panties she wore.

"Chicken korma, with basmati rice, onion bhajis, maybe a couple of samosas."

"Any salad?" she'd ask, hopefully.

"Guess I could do some as well."

"Not to worry if you weren't doing it anyway," she'd say. "See you later." And she'd be out the door, pressing buttons on that running watch of hers that looks like it's fallen off the space shuttle.

I'm a chef by trade, a couch potato by nature, and cuddly by design. Joanna is a lawyer by trade, an athlete by nature, and skinny as whipcord by design. We were total opposites, but in one of those random friend-of-a-friend-of-a-friend moments, we'd ended up as housemates.

When my girlfriend moved out, I couldn't afford to keep the town house on by myself. I needed a housemate fast.

"This is Joanna," my friend Jazz announced one evening in Kosmo's. "She's new here, works downtown and needs somewhere to live." She winked at me and murmured, "And she's one of us."

I looked her over. She was casually dressed, but with an edge of affluence that was missing from my own faded jeans, rugby shirt, and scuffed loafers. Her hair was neatly cut and obviously styled by a professional, rather than in the backyard by Jazz after one too many glasses of pink zin.

"What do you work at?" I asked.

"I'm a litigation attorney." She smiled slightly. "Please don't hold it against me."

Her smile won me over. Plus anyone as neat as her couldn't be hard to live with.

"Come around tomorrow," I instructed. "If you like the place, you can move in straight away."

Her silver Miata was outside my door before nine the next morning. It was jammed with her gear.

"I hope I'm not too early," she said. "I came straight over after my run."

I ran a hand through my spiky hair and hoped the pillow hadn't creased my face. "Sure," I mumbled, "come in." I waved a hand in the general direction of the house. "Look around while I put coffee on. Your bedroom would be the one at the top of the stairs on the left."

She took her time looking, long enough for me to not only make and drink a cup of java, but also reheat some of yesterday's potato and sweet pepper frittata and arrange smoked salmon on two plates.

She returned to the kitchen and flushed pink. "Oh, I'm sorry. I've obviously come at a bad time, if you're having company for breakfast."

I put a hand on her shoulder, pushing her onto one of the high stools at the breakfast bar. "This is for you. You have to eat, right?"

She eyed the plate. "This looks delicious."

She said it in a way that I knew she had reservations, but I ignored them and passed her the silverware. She demolished the smoked salmon, but only nibbled at the frittata, managing to pick out the vegetables, leaving the egg on the plate.

I refilled her coffee mug. "Are you allergic to eggs? I'm sorry, I should have asked."

"No, I'm just careful what I eat." She paused. "Have you decided you can't live with me because of that?"

"The room's yours if you want it. Six hundred a month, including Internet and cable, plus half the bills."

She smiled, showing slightly crooked white teeth. She was pretty, and the uneven teeth made her more interesting than if they'd been perfectly straight. Perfection is its own flaw.

"Today?" she asked, hopefully.

"Perfect! I'm cooking tonight. We can get to know each other better."

Get to know each other we did. After dinner—of which she'd picked at the roast pork, but devoured the vegetables and eaten a couple of spoonfuls of coconut pudding—we took our wine and relaxed on the couch. The TV stayed off, and we concentrated on learning about each other. We both liked sci-fi series;

Joanna even admitted that once she'd dressed as a Klingon and attended a Star Trek convention. We both were politically active for GLBT rights, and we figured out we'd been on the same same-sex marriage march to the capitol building last year.

And all the time we talked, I was mesmerized by her shiny jagged cap of hair and neat, compact figure. I was conscious of the thrum of desire building deep in my belly that said, yes, this is a gorgeous woman. One I wanted to know better. One that I wanted to kiss—and more. With her legs curled underneath her on the couch, she looked absurdly young, more a waiflike elfin child than a woman. But her long, graceful fingers curled around her wineglass confidently, and when she set her full lips to the rim and flicked a wicked glance at me from underneath her lashes, I knew this was no child.

I tried to contain my response to her. Seducing housemates has never been a good idea, even if she could possibly be interested in a cuddly blob of laziness like me. Sleeping with a housemate is a fast track to rattling around in an empty house by yourself wondering how you'll make next month's rent.

"Rule Four," I'd told Jazz one evening a couple of years ago, when I'd lost another housemate after we'd ended up in bed after Mexican food and margaritas. To me she'd been a friend with benefits; to her, I'd been The One.

"What's Rule Four?"

"Never seduce a housemate. Keep it separate."

"What are Rules One through Three?"

"No idea. I'll think of them later."

I'd had many housemates since that time, and many lovers, but since the instigation of Rule 4, they had never overlapped. And I'd never been particularly tempted—until Joanna. Joanna got to me in a way neither lovers nor housemates had. It wasn't only that she was gorgeous (and she was), it was her humor, the way she ate so healthily and carefully, but could put away a bottle of red wine with ease. It was how she'd tiptoe down the stairs to go for her run at some unearthly hour but always forget about the loose stair and curse like a sailor when it creaked. It was how she'd always wash up if I cooked. Best of all, I loved how she never lectured me on my unhealthy habits or dropped hints about exercise. Often when I'd creep in from a late shift at the restaurant where I worked, she'd be sitting on the couch in her pj's, a tumbler of red by her side, her glasses sliding down her nose and a book in her hand. She'd put down the book and pour me a glass of wine, following me as I padded around, shucking my uniform in random pieces around the house. Joanna would step over the black and white check pants without complaint, and then she'd prop herself in the doorway of my bathroom while I showered, and we'd carry on a shouted conversation over the running water.

I fantasized about her, of course. In my most persistent fantasy she didn't stay propped against the bathroom door, hidden from me by the corner and the misted shower screen. Instead she'd surprise me by opening the shower door and walking in. In my fantasy, she'd prop her ever-present glass of red on the soap holder and wind wet arms around my neck. Her clothes would cling to her, and she'd press her body to mine and kiss me without talk or explanation, simply her and me and wet, hot kisses under the shower spray.

Like one of Pavlov's dogs, every time I took a shower, I'd have to fight to keep the thoughts away. And my post-work ritual involving the shower spray and a knee-jerking climax had to stop. Because if she ever did walk in on me, I didn't want her to think she wasn't required.

We'd often go out together, especially on weekends. We had many friends in common, and of course we shared the same haunts—the city's only two dyke bars, the breakfast place on the park that did great eggs Benedict (although Joanna would scrape off the hollandaise sauce). Sunday afternoons, especially when the weather was cold and the wind threatened to carry us up and over the mountains, we'd often go to the bookstore downtown. We'd sit in the slouchy couches, one at each end, with a pile of books from the shelves and a big mug of moccachino (me) and a skinny latte (Joanna) and see who could find the most outlandish piece of prose in a book.

After a few months, it was as if Joanna had always been there with me. She was like a girlfriend in every way but one: we didn't sleep together.

"How's Rule Four going?" Jazz asked me one day as we sat out in the rear yard in the weak sunlight that comes with spring.

"Good." I took a slurp of the pink zin that Jazz likes. "Are you gonna cut my hair? It's getting a bit long."

"Are you tempted to break it?" she persisted. "Rule Four. Not your hair."

I stared up at the tree overhead, which was gaining the first fuzzy buds of spring. "Do you think I should get a dog? It would make me take some exercise."

"You'd make Joanna take it running with her," retorted Jazz. "Stop changing the subject."

I faced her. "Why do you ask? You've never cared before if I broke my rule."

Jazz hesitated, her round face earnest as she tried to explain. "It's just we never see you without Joanna. We never see Joanna without you. You're more of a couple than most couples. And... Well, if you're not going to crack onto her, there are others who would like a chance."

"You?"

"Yeah. I would. But if she's yours, Sam, then I'm not going to butt in."

I took a swallow of wine. The chill was leaving the glass and it was sickly sweet. I wrinkled my nose. "Why d'you always buy this pink stuff?"

"Why d'you drink it?" snapped Jazz. "A simple yes or no will suffice. Can I ask Joanna on a date, or will I be treading on your toes?"

"That's not a yes or no question."

A small bird hopped from the tree above my head to the windowsill. Joanna's windowsill. Who was I to cocoon her from my friends, from people who might be perfect for her, just because I liked her? She was the housemate with whom I got on the best. I shouldn't upset that by trying to worm my way into her panties—even if she'd give me a passing glance.

I chucked the rest of the pink zin into the pot of basil. "Go ahead, then. Ask her."

It was the next day before I saw Joanna. I came home from the restaurant and found her curled up in her pj's in her usual chair watching a *Star Trek* rerun. She uncurled when she saw me and ambled to the kitchen. "Want a glass of wine?"

"Sure."

"I'll bring it to you in the shower."

I headed off to the bathroom and tried in vain to quash my usual fantasy. How would Joanna get the wine to me in the shower unless she carried it in? The picture in my head of her wet and smiling, glass of wine in hand, pressing her body against mine under the shower jets as the wine diluted with shower water wouldn't leave my head. I went so far as to check that the shower cubicle was clean and free of grime before I stopped myself. Joanna wasn't mine to seduce, and I would do well to remember that.

I was washing my hair when I heard her at the bathroom door. "Wine's on the counter," she said. Her voice came from around the corner, her usual spot, propped in the doorjamb.

"Thanks. I need that tonight."

"Want me to bring it in to you?"

Her words, light, teasing, mischievous startled me so much I dropped the soap. Picking it up, I straightened and banged my head on the shower caddy and bottles of shower gel, shampoo, and facial scrub ricocheted off the shower walls.

"Hey, it's okay. No need to escape in terror. I'll stay out here." Her voice was closer, still amused.

"It's not that," I mumbled. "Just dropped the soap."

"What was so bad about your day that you need the wine?"

I considered as I soaped my stomach. What bits could I tell her? "The pastry chef dropped three dozen eggs in the cold larder. Then there was some asshole customer who sent back his salmon. 'It's obviously been reheated in the microwave,' he said. As if."

"I didn't think you even knew how to use a microwave."

I wasn't imagining it, Joanna's voice was closer. I still couldn't see her; she must be just out of sight, around the corner. "That's your domain. Microwave cooking."

Back to normal. Good one, Sam. I was proud of how even my voice was. No need to tell Joanna about the other bad bits of my day—the part that involved sitting on the back step of the restaurant kitchen, wondering if Jazz was inviting Joanna for sushi, or to the ballgame, or for a hit of tennis in the park. Wondering what Joanna would say. Whether she would accept.

I grabbed the loofah and attacked my elbows rather than think about it.

"I had a good day," said Joanna in conversational tones.

"Settled a big case at the courtroom door. Good settlement too. And I got asked out."

"Um," I said and scrubbed harder. Here it comes. I turned the water up in a vain attempt to drown out the inevitable.

"Don't you want to know who asked? It's someone we both know."

I turned my face up to the spray and closed my eyes, rinsing shampoo out of my hair. "Who?"

"Jazz."

I tried to read her voice. Was it excited? Jubilant? Complacent? But her tone was carefully nonchalant.

"Where are you going?"

"Who says I accepted?"

My eyes flew open. Her voice was definitely closer. She still wasn't visible, but she must be just around the corner. To prove my guess, I saw her slim arm snake out and grab my wine from the counter.

"If you're not going to drink this, I will. It's a rather nice shiraz. I'd hate for it to go to waste."

"I'll drink it," I mumbled. "But it's kinda difficult in the shower."

"She asked if I'd like to have a hit of tennis." A pause, and I imagined her setting her full lips to the wineglass, leaving a smear of lip balm. "I didn't know Jazz played."

"She took it up a few months ago." Jazz's reason was now very obvious. Joanna was fit and sporty; Jazz must have thought a shared interest would give her more of a chance.

"She's lost a bit of weight lately. That must be why."

"Yeah." I tried not to let the hopelessness infuse my voice. Joanna had noticed Jazz's weight loss. So there was no chance for cuddly, inactive me. Even if I were interested.

The soap slipped out of my grasp. Who was I fooling? Not

Jazz, not me. Of course I was interested. Rule 4 would be blown out the window if I had any say in it. I wanted Joanna, in my home, in my life, in my bed. I bent to pick up the soap again, hoping the running water would cover my heavy sigh. I'd had my chance when Jazz had asked if I minded, and I'd blown it. Now I just had to minimize the damage, not let Joanna know, not make it awkward for Jazz.

"So when are you going?" I asked. "There's a nice sushi place near the courts, you could go there afterward."

"Who says I'm going on a date?" Her footsteps sounded on the tiles. "Sam, if you're not going to drink this wine, I'm going to finish it. Which would be a pity, as I poured it for you."

And then her figure appeared around the corner, glass of wine in her hand, half-smile on her face. She opened the shower door and paused, considering.

Oh God. My fantasy, so close yet so far. I tried for nonchalance. Holding the loofah in what I hoped was a suitably casual pose down over my pussy, I reached for the glass with the other hand. "Thanks."

Instead of handing the glass over, she took another sip. My eyes fixed on the smear of lip balm she had indeed left behind.

"I like Jazz. She's funny, and kind and good to be with. I'm flattered she asked me."

"And she's sporty and is looking pretty good."

"Do you think that's what I'm looking for? Someone like me? Oh!" She clapped a hand over her mouth. "That came out wrong. I'm not saying I look good."

"You look great. I've always thought that." The old Sam would have said that. The Sam who was Joanna's buddy and housemate would have offered the compliment without hesitation.

Joanna's eyes raked boldly up and down my body, and my

breath caught in my throat. "You look pretty good yourself right now."

"I have love handles."

Her eyes settled on my hips, revealed by the inadequate loofah I still held. "You have curves. Not handles. I like curves."

If this were any other woman, I would have taken that as a blatant come-on. An invitation. But in our months of living together, Joanna and I had fallen into a comfortable routine. It wasn't the first time she'd complimented me on how I looked, but it was the first time she'd said it in quite that tone of voice: low, caressing, almost a purr. As if she were stroking my skin with her words. I wondered how much wine she'd had.

"I need to exercise more. I have muscles underneath this padding. It's about time I found them."

"I think you're fine, just the way you are. Cuddly bits and all."

The conversation was moving into the surreal. It would move into the bizarre if she said she didn't want to go out with Jazz, she wanted me. Or if she acted on my fantasy and stepped into the cubicle.

Joanna took a big breath and the wineglass trembled in her hand, its contents vibrating like soft-baked meringue. "Jazz is lovely, and I'm going to meet her for tennis sometime. And she did ask me for sushi afterward, but I said no. She wanted a for-real date, with kisses, and maybe sex, and a relationship up for grabs."

I held my breath. There was a "but" in there somewhere, I could hear it in her voice.

"I told her it wasn't fair. That I'd fallen in love with someone else."

I clutched the loofah tightly. The way she was saying the words—softly, as if she were a little afraid—made me hope.

"Thing is, the person I've fallen in love with likes me. I know she does. We do everything together. But she's got this stupid rule—"

"It is a stupid rule." My voice sounded unnaturally loud in the shower cubicle, even over the rushing water.

"Is it?"

I could see her face, her eyes huge, but brave, meeting mine without hesitation. "Rules are made to be broken. Jo—"

And then I couldn't continue, because the shower door opened wider, and suddenly she was in the shower with me, that stupid wineglass clutched tightly in her hand. The water poured over our heads, sluicing our bodies. Her pj's were wet, and she laughed, a free and clear sound, and then she was in my arms and red wine spilled down my back as she wrapped her arms around my neck in a stranglehold and her lips crashed onto mine. The kiss was hot, and above all wet. Very wet. She tasted of shiraz and laughter. My hands roamed her body, exactly as in my fantasy, learning her shape, how she felt under my hands. The crashing noise in my head was the sound of Rule 4 smashing into a million tiny pieces.

NOTE TO SELF

Geneva King

Note to Self: You've been set up on a blind date with your ex. Your dating life is officially shot to hell.

"Danielle?"

"Kizzy?"

We stare at each other for an uncomfortable minute. It'd taken me six long months to get over our breakup, and even then I'd had to convince myself I'd really been dating Satan in disguise.

If she is the devil, she's gotten a serious makeover. No snarling fangs curl from her gums or pointy horns rise from her scalp. I can only see the front of her, but I'd wager there's no leathery tail protruding from her backside either.

Instead, she looks gorgeous, more proof that life is sublimely unfair.

Her face breaks into a smile and she envelops me in a hug. "Darling, it is so good to see you! How have you been?"

Darling? And why is she talking like she's afraid of contractions? A year ago, *y'alls* had decorated her speech like gaudy jewelry. I hug her back, trying to ignore the scent that engulfs me. It smells expensive. And good.

"Well." Now that we've observed the niceties, I'm not sure what to do. "I've already got a table."

She beams and I notice her chipped tooth is no more. Actually, everything in her mouth looks a bit...straighter. Whiter too.

"We should eat. Besides, I want to catch up."

This is a bit too weird. I know the lesbian social network is small, but give me a break.

Note to Self: Kill Merrill.

"Do you go by Jessalyn now?"

Kizzy/Jessalyn nods. "I thought it was more professional. Kizzy sounds so backwoods country."

I watch her examine the menu, her straightened hair falling over her face. She looks angelic. Suddenly, I can't remember why it didn't work out with her.

"I wonder how the salads are. Do you know what you're getting?"

"I hear the burgers are really good."

Her nose wrinkles. "You'll never lose those last ten pounds if you keep eating like that."

Now I remember. Satan in disguise.

After dinner, we walk out of the restaurant together. When we reach my car, we stand around, arms folded, looking everywhere but at each other.

"Well, it was nice seeing you again."

"You want to come home with me?"

We speak at the same time, so it takes me a moment to register her question. Go home with her? Is she serious?

I shake my head. "I don't think that'd be very smart. But thanks for asking."

She snorts. "Who said anything about smart?" She steps

close. "I'm asking if you want to come back to my place and have some no-strings-attached fun. Like we used to." She presses me against the car and kisses me like we're already in bed and not in a crowded parking lot.

When she pulls away, my knees are shaking. "Ah. Fun. You should've said."

She grins. "I'll meet you there." She gives me another kiss. "Don't keep me waiting."

Note to Self: Ex-sex is the best sex. Ever.

I share this insight with Raquel and Merrill the next time we go out. Happy hour used to be my and Raquel's tradition, but once she started dating Merrill, we became a threesome. And lately, Merrill's been pushing me to find a fourth, hence the run-in with Kizzy.

"Well, was it good?" Merrill leans forward, her eyes bright with curiosity.

Raquel slaps her arm. "It doesn't matter! She fucked Pyscho Kizzy." She turns her wrath back on me. "What were you thinking? You should have left as soon as she walked up."

Truthfully, I'd been thinking that it had been a while since I'd had another girl in my bed, something Raquel doesn't know much about. Part of me wanted to show Jessalyn née Kizzy what a fabulous girl she missed out on. Another piece of me had melted when I saw her and couldn't remember why Raquel had to steal my phone so I wouldn't keep calling her. Raquel was great during that whole ordeal. So supportive, staying up with me until late at night, always there with a friendly hug and a kind word.

Now she doesn't look so accommodating. "I hope it was worth it."

A memory surfaces of Kizzy's face between my legs. Fucking amazing, but somehow I don't think that's what she wants to hear.

Merrill lights a cigarette. "Hey, I'm sorry. I didn't know. I thought you two would hit it off." She takes a deep drag. "Next time I'll do better."

Not only do I not want her to set me up with anybody she knows ever again, but I have my own suspicions about why she's so hot for me to get a date. Before I can speak, Raquel cuts me off.

"I thought you were quitting?"

Merrill shrugs and takes a puff. "I've been quitting all day. It's time for a break." She winks at me.

Raquel slumps back in her seat, arms folded. I know that look, she's pissed. "Merrill, we talked about this. You promised."

"Damn it, it is one fucking cigarette."

"It's always one fucking cigarette!"

And they're off in another of their excessively dramatic arguments. I sip my drink and try to pretend I'm invisible, like I'm not really watching the hurt spread across my best friend's face as she pleads with Merrill, who's storming away from the table.

"I'm sorry. I didn't mean to start a fight in front of you." She puts her face in her hands and starts to cry.

It's not like I haven't seen it before. "It's okay." I slide in next to her and wrap my arm around her shoulders.

She looks up at me, runny mascara streaking her cheeks. She's saying something, but I only notice how brown her eyes are, how she bites her lips when she's upset. How soft her mouth must be.

She wipes her face and I snap out of it. "Honestly, sometimes I wonder where we're really going. I mean, all we do is argue and make up and fight again. What kind of a relationship is that?"

It's on the tip of my tongue to tell her to dump Merrill on her ass and find someone new, preferably me, but my sensible side keeps still. Instead, I shrug noncommittally.

Merrill comes back to the table, fresh drinks in hand. "I'm sorry, baby."

Raquel sniffs, looking at her girlfriend. "Me too."

"I really am trying. I just get tense."

"I know. I should be more supportive."

"I love you." Merrill kisses her temple. "You're the only girl for me, you know that."

"I love you too."

"Will you dance with me?"

Raquel nods and follows her to the dance floor. I repress the urge to gag, instead plastering a smile on my face. They look so close on the floor, I'm envious. I wish it were my hands resting on Raquel's bottom, my chin that her head snuggles into. But Merrill's the one holding her and I'm left cradling the purses.

Note to self: Get over Raquel. For real this time.

My vow to move on from Raquel lasts about as long as Merrill's promise to quit smoking. It'd be easier if Raquel weren't my best friend and we didn't do everything together.

"Okay, how about this one?"

The dress looks the same as the first three she tried on. "It's fine. Just pick something, please."

She examines herself in the mirror. "I don't look fat in this?"

"No, you're perfect."

"Merrill told me I should lay off the dessert for a while."

"Merrill's a bitch." And a blind one at that.

She smiles. "I knew you'd say that. Hang on. I have one more I want to try."

"Just hurry up." I'm almost out of magazines and my foot's fallen asleep.

"Hey, I know that last date was a disaster, but I think I found someone you'll really like."

Jeez, not her too. "Could you two stop trying to set me up? I can find my own dates."

Her voice sounds muffled. "I know. I just want to see you happy."

Then stop fucking around with Merrill and notice me! Shit, does that sound as pathetic as I think it does?

"Ta-da! What do you think?"

I can't answer her immediately. I'm too busy checking out the way the thin material drapes over her full curves. Merrill's an idiot if she doesn't appreciate how gorgeous Raquel is.

"That's the dress."

"Sweet!" She twirls around the room. "That's a relief; I was beginning to think I wasn't going to find anything to wear." She pulls me off the bed and drags me with her. "You are truly the best friend a girl could ever have."

I'm thankful I'm not a guy, because right about now I'd be trying to find a textbook to hide behind. As it is, my pulse feels like a runaway train and I've started to sweat from the exertion of appearing unaffected.

"Seriously, Dani. I don't know what I'd do without you. I don't want you to find a girlfriend. It's selfish, I know. I keep thinking, what'll happen to me when you find that special girl and you're no longer around when I need you?"

I pull her close to me and give her a hug. "I'll always be there for you." I lean back and look her in the eyes. "Always."

She pushes the stray hairs from my face, a contemplative look on her face. I can't breathe, much less move. All I see is her mouth come toward mine, then suddenly I feel the brush of her lips. Soft. Sweet. Tender.

We kiss again. Firmly. Urgently. Her fingers entwine in my hair, my hands caressing her back as her tongue explores my mouth.

Still, my brain won't totally let me enjoy the moment. "Raquel—"

She silences me with a tug at my shirt. "Take it off."

Note to Self: When the girl you've been lusting after forever wants to fuck you, shut up and let her.

And so I strip, falling into her on the bed, loving the way her body feels against me, a bundle of creamy brown curves pressed against my flesh. The heat of her cunt warming my thigh as she straddles me. She hasn't shed the dress and I don't want her to. I want to fuck her in the dress that was meant for Merrill, the dress that the self-centered bitch wouldn't be able to appreciate, make her come and leave my mark on it so that every time she wears it, she'll think of me.

I loosen the top enough so her breasts spill out and grasp a nipple between my lips. She moans and leans closer until I'm almost smothered by the flesh pressed against my face. Her hardened nubs occupy my mouth as my hands sneak under the skirt to explore her body. My nails scratch a trail down her slightly rounded stomach, until she grunts and shoves my hand farther down. Already, the heat from her pussy warms my hands and the merest stroke leaves my finger covered with her juice.

With great reluctance, I leave her lip-gloss-streaked nipples and lay her down on the bed. "Come here," I whisper.

Her eyes close as I kneel before her splayed body. I open her lips gently and inhale her earthy scent as arousal washes over me. My finger slips easily inside and as she opens her legs farther, I add another and caress her from the inside. I'm torn. I want to draw it out, tease her the way she's been teasing me all these months, but then she moans my name and I can't make her wait any longer.

She tastes like ambrosia and I suck at her clit like I'm receiving sustenance from the gods themselves. All too soon, she's tensing and shuddering. She grasps my free hand as the orgasm hits her. I crawl next to her and kiss her soft mouth, wondering what happens next. Wanting her to touch me before she snaps back to reality and the dream has to end.

I needn't have worried. She squeezes my ass and then straddles me, kissing a trail down my spine.

"Dani." Her hand makes its way between my legs, stroking me where I need it most.

"Now. Please." I push my hips up toward her until I feel her tongue make contact with my cunt.

That's the last we speak until we collapse, spent, next to each other and drift off, limbs entwined. When I wake, she's still sleeping and the dress is twisted around her waist. Reluctantly, I slip out of bed and pull the covers around her neck. The reality of the situation is starting to sink in. It's amazing how clear and ugly things become after an orgasm.

Note to Self: When your best friend decides to fuck you in a moment of insanity, don't do it. Seriously. Not a good idea.

Three days later, my phone rings. It's Raquel. It's the first I've heard from her since The Incident. Even though I've tried to call her, I just chicken out and hang up. What would I say anyhow? Sorry for jumping you, I couldn't resist your tits in that gown? Any way you put it, it comes off bad.

"Hello?"

"I'm downstairs. I want to come in." There's no warmth to her command, so I hit the buzzer and wait for her to come to the door.

She looks pissed. "Hi," I offer tentatively.

"Next time leave cash."

"What?"

"Next time you fuck me and run out without having the

decency to say good-bye, leave some money on the dresser."

"I…I didn't know what to say." It sounds lame even to my ears.

"Bye. Thanks for the sex. I lo— I don't know, anything."

"I'm sorry."

She folds her arms and stares at me. "I know."

I don't know if she's referring to my apology or me. "We made a mistake?"

"Did we?"

Did we? What kind of question is that? And then I'm reminded of my drama with Kizzy, the constant push-pull, fuck me, fuck you power struggle. I don't want to go through that with Raquel. "I don't know, Raquel. It's your relationship, you tell me. You're the one with a girlfriend."

"I know."

"I just know that you're my best friend. And what happened… we never should have crossed that line. Look, we've always said we never wanted to be those girls that constantly hook up with their friends."

She sighs. "Yeah."

"So, let's not do that now."

"I thought maybe you…I don't know, maybe I'm imagining things."

No, she's not. I know it, but I'm too chickenshit to say it, even though it's almost cruel to deny her the validation she's looking for.

We look at each other for a long minute, our gaze saying everything we can't bring ourselves to put into words.

Finally, she looks away. "So it was a fluke."

"Heat of the moment."

"Completely out of our system." She looks at me slyly. "It was pretty hot."

I shrug. She looks offended. "You don't think so?"

"Eh. Why else do you think I snuck out?"

She slapped my arm and we burst into laughter, pretending to be past that awkwardness and back to our natural rhythm.

"Want to go to happy hour with us?"

"Pass." So not interested in watching her cuddle with Merrill. "Next time, I promise."

"Okay." She looks sad. She gives me a hug, our usual good-bye ritual, but this time our bodies seem stuck together. Her heart thuds against my chest and I feel her hair brush against my cheek as she turns her face into me.

We stand there, mouths inches apart, for an indeterminably long period of time. One kiss can't possibly hurt, right?

"Dani?"

Carefully and reluctantly, I push her away. "Merrill's waiting for you."

She nods and gropes for her purse. "Bye, Dani."

And then she goes, leaving me alone in my tiny kitchen.

A week later, I still haven't made it to happy hour or any of our other usual hangouts. Worse, Raquel hasn't come to drag me out either. But Kizzy hasn't been so silent.

"Dani? Hi, it's Jessalyn. Well, Kizzy, I guess we know each other too well for that. Anyhow, I had a great time with you last week and I was hoping we can do it again soon. Movie, coffee, it's up to you. Call me."

Delete. Next message.

"Dani, it's me again. I know you're busy, but I'd really like to see you again. I just keep thinking about you and I realized...I still love you. I was stupid to let you go. Call me, please."

I hit the Erase button so forcefully the machine clatters against the counter. Is this how my life is going to turn out? Doomed to fall for women when they're emotionally or logistically unavailable only for the affection to be returned when I no longer want it?

Note to Self: Women have an innate ability to sense when your life is at its shittiest and pick that time to make it worse.

The phone rings. I recognize Merrill's number. With a sigh, I pick up.

"Hello?"

"I want you to come to dinner tonight. I've got a surprise for Raquel and I know she'll want you to share the day with us."

My stomach drops. Surprise? That doesn't sound like anything good.

"Yeah, I guess I can come out."

"Great! I'm so nervous. I just want everything to be perfect. It's at Mari's at seven. I've got a table."

"Mari's, seven," I repeat dutifully.

"Oh, can you pick her up and bring her?"

"Sure. Merrill, what's the surprise?"

She laughs. "I'm not gonna say. Let's just say, if all goes well, you'll be helping her pick out a new set of china. Oh, and don't worry, I've got something for you too." The phone clicks off.

China? The only time I know people waste money on that is for— The word floats in my mind like a caricature bubble. Marriage? Merrill and Raquel? My Raquel? No fucking way!

Note to Self: Fuck!!!

Raquel and I pull into Mari's at exactly seven. She's been talking about something, but I haven't been able to focus. I don't know what to say, but I can't let her go without one last attempt to make things right.

Finally, she notices something's off. "What's the matter?"

"Nothing. Everything. Are you in love with Merrill?"

"What? Dani, what's going on?"

I straighten up and look her in the eye. "Just answer me. I

need to know. More importantly, if you go in there, you need to know."

"What the hell are you talking about?"

"I can't tell you."

She folds her arms and gives me The Look. I take a deep breath. "Merrill's going to propose."

"What?" She looks at me incredulously. "Don't play with me."

"I'm serious."

"She said that? She actually said marriage?"

"Well, no, not in so many words. But it was pretty damn clear."

She sits back in the seat. "Oh."

I'm puzzled as to her lack of outrage and then it hits me. "You're not seriously considering it?"

"Why shouldn't I?"

What kind of question is that? "Because she's all wrong for you! And you know it."

"I know that she doesn't hide her feelings from me, no matter what they are. Is it love? Who knows? It's not perfect, but at least I know where I stand with her."

I don't miss the barb. "That sounds...pathetic, if you want to know the truth."

"I don't think you're one to talk about pathetic."

I grab her arm as she fumbles for the latch. "At least I'm trying here."

She whips back around. "Trying to what? What exactly are you trying to do?"

My tongue feels stuck and I'm struck silent by the force of her anger.

"That's what I thought." With a last venomous look, she hops out of my car and disappears inside, leaving me banging my head against the steering wheel.

I make it inside in time to see Merrill kissing Raquel hello. When they break apart, Raquel sits in the chair Merrill pulls out for her and starts examining the menu.

"Hi, Dani." A silky voice startles me. I turn around and come face-to-face with Kizzy.

"What are you doing here?" I don't have it in me to be polite, but she doesn't seem to notice.

"Merrill invited me," she purrs as she kisses my cheek. She looks at the couple talking at the table. "They're so sweet, aren't they?"

So is sugar, until it gives you diabetes. "Um, sure."

She slips her well-manicured hand in mine and snuggles against me. "I think that could be us one day."

I snort. We were them at one point. And that's why we're no longer an Us.

She must have mistaken my reaction because she turns to face me, a serious look in her eye. "I know we didn't work out before, but I want another chance. I'm such a different person now. I know we can have something special."

I start to speak, but she presses a finger against my lips. "You don't have to answer now. Just think about it."

I catch the approving glint in Merrill's eye and pull away from Kizzy. Raquel's studying the menu, but her face isn't as friendly as it was moments before. For some reason, my spirits lift just a little.

We sit down and Merrill reaches for her glass. "Now that we're all here, I want to make an announcement."

Here it comes, the moment of truth. My stomach feels tight and I wonder if I'm going to be physically ill.

"As you know, Raquel and I have been together for eighteen months now. And they've been the happiest months of my life."

She pauses dramatically to beam at Raquel, who I'm pleased to see looks as ill as I feel.

Merrill takes a deep breath before continuing. "I love you and I want us to take the next step." She pulls a box out of her pocket and places it gently on the table. Raquel stares at it hypnotically as Merrill lowers herself to one knee.

Beside me, Kizzy squeeze my arm. "Here it comes."

"Raquel, I want—"

"Don't do it!"

It takes a moment before I realize the words came out of my mouth. And now that everyone is staring at me, I can't take it back. And I can't ignore it.

My mouth feels like a desert and I'm super aware of my heart thudding in my chest. Half of me wants to curl up and die, but the other half is bitch-slapping me, daring me to grow a backbone and fight for the woman I love before it's too late.

"So maybe you're right. I'm not the most open or demonstrative person." Once I start talking, the words seem to trip over themselves to come out. "And I totally fucked things up between us and I know what you wanted to hear in my kitchen and I was too chicken to say it because I didn't want to fuck everything up between us...and I guess that didn't work 'cause I wouldn't be here and I know you totally don't owe me anything, even listening to me now, but I am asking, begging you. Don't marry Merrill."

"What the hell is going on?"

From the corner of my eye, I see Merrill push back from the table. She looks pissed, but I'm only focused on Raquel, who's staring back at me.

"Danielle?" Kizzy whimpers, but I shake her arm off mine.

"I love you, Raquel. Seriously. I always have."

"Raquel, what the hell is this?" Merrill demands.

Raquel opens her mouth, but nothing comes out. Finally, she manages an "I don't know what to say."

"Well, I do." Merrill jerks up so quickly I think she might hit me, but instead she throws some money on the table. "Don't think I didn't know you were after my girl. Fuck, Dani, this is pathetic, even for you. Grow up and stay the fuck away from us."

She starts to storm out, muttering something I can't hear, and tugs Raquel's arm. Kizzy sweeps behind them with a scathing backwards glance. "So selfish," she mutters, her beautiful face twisted in a scowl. Even worse, I can feel everyone else in the restaurant watching us, like we're some characters in a bad play.

"She's right, you know."

Raquel speaks so quietly, at first I think I imagined it.

Merrill stops in the middle of her tirade to stare at her lover. "Raquel, what are you saying?"

Raquel's eyes lock with mine as she frees herself from Merrill's grasp. "She's right about us. We'd never work out. We hardly do now."

"Wait, what? You can't be serious. You're leaving me? Because she made some stupid public speech?" Merrill seems caught between anger and confusion as she stares at Raquel.

"No, this has nothing to do with her. We're just not meant to be." She turns to face her now-ex. "I'm sorry, Merrill. I should have said something ages ago."

Merrill looks back and forth between us, then shakes her head and throws up her hand. "Whatever, bitch. This is so not worth it. Come on, Jess, let's go."

That leaves me and Raquel together in the middle of the restaurant, staring at each other.

"Impressive speech."

I can't tell if she's angry or not. "I meant every word."

She tilts her head as if she's considering me, then gives me the first smile of the evening. "You owe me a ride."

My heart speeds up as I step toward her. "I'll take you wherever you want to go."

Our mouths meet and I kiss her like we're the only people in the room. The patrons, waitresses, everybody has faded away. I try to put everything I'm thinking and feeling into the kiss and I think she understands because she's giving everything back to me.

"Take me home," she whispers as we break apart. "Now."

I stroke my beautiful Raquel's cheek and grab my purse. "As you wish."

Note to Self: Sometimes, just sometimes, things actually work out in your favor after all.

Note to Self: New relationship loving beats ex-sex any day.

A TIME AND MATERIALS JOB

Anna Watson

I like going into homes early in the morning. Usually kids are just waking up, parents are making breakfast, and it always smells good. Sometimes people are doing a whole bang-up breakfast—bacon, eggs, pancakes, the works—and sometimes it's just coffee and toast, but it always smells friendly and cozy, full of life and family.

Her house was completely breakfastless, though. No cocoa on the stove, no oatmeal bubbling, no glasses of juice on the table. Her two little girls, about ten and seven, were standing in the hall with their backpacks on, fighting in low, tired voices.

"I know math about an infinity better than you!" The older one's auburn hair was held off her face by two barrettes made out of blue ribbon. "You don't even know two plus two, you're such a baby, you're so fat."

"Nuh-uh, I do so know. And plus also, I'm a way better speller than you, you can't even spell, you couldn't even spell *variety*, come on, try and spell it, I know you can't!" The younger one, with her curly strawberry-blond hair, jounced her Hello Kitty backpack aggressively and glared at her sister.

"Can so. V, e, r…"

"Loser! Loser!"

Their mom glanced over at them wearily and said, "Girls, please stop. I know you're hungry, but we'll pick up a bagel on the way to school."

The kids shut up for a moment to look at her, then started back in, even more nastily. I saw the older one pinch the younger one. They weren't at their best right now, but I thought they looked like pretty nice kids.

"Please just go ahead and start," she told me, taking her car keys from a basket on the hall table. "You have my cell?"

I nodded, smiling, and watched them leave, the girls still going at it. Then I got to work. She had a great 1930s bungalow—she'd just bought it, and there were still boxes everywhere—but she was worried about the wiring and I was impatient to see what we were up against. I was alone today because Randy, my apprentice, had the flu. I started in the attic, pulling up floorboards and beginning to map things out. I've found the most interesting things under attic floorboards, like old pictures, vintage toys, desiccated food, and this attic was no exception. I set aside an old hat pin, a wooden puzzle piece with half a daisy painted on it, and a metal soldier with the paint rubbed off—I guess he was probably made out of lead. Usually homeowners get a kick out of seeing that stuff.

Even though it's dirty and can be frustrating, I love rewiring old houses. It's highly personally satisfying to make a house safe for a family. It's funny, because people go around baby-proofing like crazy, making their kids wear helmets to ride their tricycles, but never give the wiring of their houses a second thought. I always tell people, "Take electricity seriously! It could save your life. " I was humming to myself, getting to the heart of the matter, which was, as I'd suspected, a lot of knob and tube shit as old as the house, when I heard the front door open downstairs. I thought she would call up to me, see how it was going, but the phone rang just as she came in. I heard her answer.

I never work with a radio on the way a lot of electricians do. I figure you're already in someone's intimate space, knocking through walls, poking and prying, all obnoxious with your presence and power tools, so there's no need to add insult to injury by cranking Melissa Etheridge or whatever. So I could hear her voice clearly coming up through the laid-open attic floor.

She was talking to a lawyer and she was really upset.

"But he knows the girls do better with the other schedule!" she was saying, and it sounded like she was trying not to cry. I kept working, but I couldn't help hearing the whole conversation. Maybe I wanted to hear it. I heard her start to cry halfway through and keep on crying after she hung up. In fact, I finally turned on the drill, even though I didn't need it, just to give her some privacy. When I turned it off, her car door was slamming and then she drove off. I looked over at the little clutch of things I was keeping to show her. I'd just added an exchange—a junction where the wires meet. Some previous owner, some Mr. Fix It, had done his own wiring, and how he'd done it is he'd kept it all nice and neat and modern-looking anyplace you could see it, but back inside the walls where it's hidden, he'd sloppily spliced new wires onto old, a total safety disaster. At this particular junction, the wire had shot a spark. You could see the little charred place on the metal. Lucky for whoever was in the house at the time, the wire had jumped back and hadn't started a fire. But it could have. It sure could have.

The next morning, it was the same thing. The tired, angry kids, the sad-eyed mama. She sure was beautiful, though. She had that alabaster skin with a sprinkling of freckles, big ones, that probably used to embarrass her when she was a kid. Her eyes were brown with these almost-transparent lashes. The first time I met her, she was wearing mascara, but today she'd forgotten, or just not bothered, and the way it looked, it made her eyes seem really vulnerable, not to have that barrier. If you looked closely, you could see her lashes, delicate and pale. Fluttery. The most amazing thing, though, was her hair, this curly, frizzy, thick, alive mass of red hair. Not just red, but all shades of red, I mean, from golden and bronze to dark auburn. A person could get lost in hair like that.

That day, she didn't come home after she left with the kids, but the lawyer called mid-morning, and because she had the volume up on the answering machine, I could hear what he said. I went and turned the thing down as soon as I could get there, but from what I heard, it didn't sound too good. It sounded like her ex was a real motherfucker, is what it sounded like.

The next day, Randy was back on the job, and things went a lot more quickly. She's a wiry, skinny little dyke and can get back into crawl spaces better than me. I'm a butch of substance, or at least that's what my last girlfriend called me. Big around and tall, too, which helped when I was coming up in the trade, I mean with guys who didn't like women who wanted to be electricians. Or maybe just didn't like women, period, and for sure not gay ones. Well, sometimes it helped because they'd keep their distance. Other times it was like it pissed them off even more that I wasn't small and dainty or whatever, and they were even shittier to me than ever. Fuck them, though, because I'm a better electrician than they'll ever be.

Friday when she came home—Maeve, that is, that's her name—Randy and I were working in the girls' bedroom, surrounded by Polly Pockets and stuffed animals. This bungalow rewiring was turning into a lot of work, which I had told her at the beginning it could. I told her this one was a time and materials job and that I wouldn't have a very good idea of any of it—how long it would take, how much it would cost—until I got under the floor and into the walls to see what we were dealing with. She said that was fine and didn't kick up a fuss the way some people do. Trying to boss you around, thinking they know something about it. Maeve said she was prepared for whatever it cost, that she was determined to make the house safe. She seemed to trust me and Randy, and plus, she was interested, even though she was obviously going through a hard time. I took her around Friday afternoon and showed her everything we were doing. She asked great questions and got a kick out of looking into the walls and seeing the insides of her new house. At one point, I brushed against her when I was handing her the fixture I mentioned earlier, where the wire sparked, and afterward in the truck when we were driving away, Randy was messing with me, saying I got all red in the face. I punched her on the arm and told her to mind her business, but it was true. Being so close to that beautiful, hurting woman was doing something to me.

Monday morning, the girls weren't there. When I asked her about it, she turned even paler than usual and tears came up in her eyes.

"They're with their dad this week," she whispered, and I could have kicked my own ass all the way around the block. What was the matter with me? It was just I somehow wanted to let her know I liked her kids, that I thought they were cute, but here I was just helping her heart break even more. Seeing that raw, desperate pain on her face, I just about lost it. I wanted to help her so bad. I know it's corny as hell, but I wanted to rewire her heart the way I was rewiring the house, put in good, clean, safe wire where old, faulty, dangerous ones had been.

I started to tear up a little, too. She saw and gave a little laugh.

"Do you have kids?" she asked. So I told her about being with Alison, who I guess you would call my first wife. We were together six years, and I helped her raise her little boy, Mason, right up until she fell out of love with me and kicked me to the curb. She still let me see Mason, though, and he and I are still tight. I even learned how to text on my damn cell phone so we could stay in touch now that he's in college. That made her laugh, and we talked about technology for a little bit, and then she started telling me about her girls, Kiera and Laney. Randy came back from a supplies run, took one look, and just clumped upstairs. I would have to join her pretty soon, but I liked watching Maeve talk about her babies. I liked how her face flushed and her eyes lost a little bit of their sadness. She was telling me about how Laney, the younger one, loved animals so much that she used to dig in the garden to find earthworms to kiss and how Maeve had been worried she would get some weird disease from it. I was laughing, thinking about that little curly-headed toddler smacking on those worms, when Maeve shook her head and looked up at me.

"I'm keeping you from your work," she said. I wanted to reach out and touch her cheek, but I just shoved my hands in my pockets and shrugged. She said she had to make a phone call and I went upstairs to join Randy, who smiled at me and shook her head, biting back some joking remark, I could tell. She knew how lonely I'd been since the last woman I'd been dating turned out to be one of those polyamory lesbians and told me she wanted to start seeing someone else along with me. Live and let live, is what I say, but I guess I'm old-fashioned when it comes to myself—monogamous and all that. We parted on good terms, but like I said, I'd been lonely. I'm not that good all on my own. I like to have someone to relax with at the end of the day, someone to spoil, someone I can talk about the world with. And here I was falling for a straight woman. A beautiful, brokenhearted straight woman.

Which is why I choked on my beer when Randy and I spotted Maeve dancing by herself at Women's Night at the local gay bar a few months later. We'd finished the job a long time ago, and I'd managed to completely fail to ask her out. I'd wanted to call her, many times, but I never managed to dial. Usually, I'm not so shy, but I guess I was so worried that she would say no, let me down gently in a nice, straight-lady way, that I just couldn't get myself to do it.

Randy smacked my shoulder and gave me a double thumbs up. My heart had started pounding the moment I saw her, but I tried to play it cool.

"She's probably here with a man," I told Randy, wiping foam off my chin. "Slumming or something."

Randy laughed. "I don't think so," she said. "I think she's sitting with her." She gestured to another really femmey woman who was at the bar flirting with the bartender, a virile, tattooed number with about a thousand piercings.

"Do you think they're together?" I asked. Now my stomach was hurting, too. Randy laughed again.

"Somehow I doubt it," she said, still looking over at the bar. I looked back over there just in time to see the bartender lock lips with the femme and not come up for air for a long time.

"Yes!" Randy and I said together, clinking glasses. I looked out on the dance floor and found Maeve again. She was dancing kind of self-consciously, but there was also an excitement about her, an electricity. I wondered if she'd ever been to a gay bar before.

"Well, go ask the lady for a dance!" urged Randy. "What are you waiting for?"

I was just waiting, I guess, prolonging the moment, watching Maeve close her eyes and lean into the beat, the colored lights flickering over her sweet face. I was waiting, just watching her spin and boogie.

The song ended and she opened her eyes, searching for her friend, who was still kissing the bartender. Sometimes I wonder how that girl keeps her job. I got up and waved, gesturing to the chair beside me Randy had hastily vacated.

Maeve came over, out of breath from dancing, and gave me a kiss on the cheek. Her lips were very soft.

"The girls were just asking about you this morning," she said, sitting in Randy's chair. She picked up a napkin and fanned herself. "It's hot out there!"

"How are they?" I asked. "How are you?"

Her smile wavered and she reached out to touch my hand. "Thirsty," she murmured.

By the time I'd gotten her some white wine and a water, she was cheerful again, and told me that Laney had gotten a lot of books out of the library about animals and was studying up to be a vet and that Kiera had started karate and was loving it. I couldn't stop smiling, listening to her. She leaned closer to me so that I could hear her over the music, and a stray wisp of hair brushed my cheek. She stopped talking and just looked at me. I wondered if my intense need to bury my face in that hair showed in my eyes.

"Maeve!" Her friend came over and joined us, full of curiosity about me and bursting with the news that she had a date with the bartender. That particular young Casanova took home so many willing females that I would hardly have called it a coup, but I didn't say anything, just introduced myself, and Randy, too, who had reappeared. Randy gave me a "well, I tried" look, and I shrugged, but it didn't matter that Maeve and I weren't alone anymore. Just sitting there with her was enough. It turned out the friend, Trisha, used to work at the co-op with Randy, so they had a lot to talk about. I asked Maeve if she wanted to dance.

"Just for a little while," she said. "I only have the babysitter until eleven."

I held out my hand to her and led her onto the dance floor. It seemed only natural not to let go, but to hold her close to me. She laid her head on my shoulder and I could feel her sigh.

"It's so nice to see you, Maeve," I said into her ear. She nodded her head, and we danced slow to something fast. At ten thirty, I asked her if I could give her a ride home, sending a silent thank-you to Randy, who does almost as well as the bartender when it comes to picking up women and so always insists on taking two cars when we go out together. Maeve and I said our good-byes, and I escorted her out to the truck. She scooched over close to me in the cab and we held hands all the way back, clasping and unclasping them whenever I had to change gears. It was so much like high school that we got the giggles. Back at her house, she invited me in, and I went to the kitchen for water while she paid the babysitter and went upstairs to check on the girls.

There was something different about the house. Maybe because it was night, maybe because they had been living there for a while now and were completely unpacked, but there was a cozy feel to the place, and I smiled to see cereal bowls and juice glasses in the sink, left over from breakfast. When she came down, she caught me looking under the shades of her living room lamps.

"How are these energy-efficient bulbs working out for you?" I asked, blushing a little.

"Just fine." She reached over me and turned the lamp off, leaving the room lit only by a streetlight outside. "Just they take so long to warm up—I'm used to turning on the light and having it be bright right away."

"I know, but you get used to it, and—" But then she was kissing me and my fingers were tangled in her hair.

"I wanted to," she whispered. "I wanted to when you were working here."

"I thought you were straight," I blurted out, then kissed her again in embarrassment. Her lips were so soft and she gave me her mouth, letting me slip my tongue inside, meeting it with her own, generously yielding to me.

"I don't think so," she said breathlessly when we stopped, and we both started laughing. "I mean, I'm not a hundred percent sure." We laughed even harder.

"Shh!" She turned on a light and listened for a moment. "They're still asleep," she said, sighing. "They would go crazy if they knew you were here. They would insist on getting up and saying hi."

"Maybe I could come back when they're awake," I said, and she nodded, settling into my arms.

"I wanted to call you," I said quietly, stroking her cheek. "I picked up the phone about a million times."

"I wanted to call you, too," she said. "But I was too shy. I've never asked a woman on a date."

"Are we on a date?" I asked, my lips brushing her ear, moving on to brush the side of her neck, find her mouth again.

"Definitely." We kissed for a long time. I wondered if maybe she would ask me to stay the night, and I wondered if I would. I was incredibly turned on, but I wasn't really in a hurry. The thought of seeing her naked made my heart stop, but I didn't need that to happen right away, and in fact, I was happy to wait. Kissing her luscious mouth, tracing the contours of her face, playing with her gorgeous hair, and nibbling her earlobe—

wasn't there enough right here to keep me busy for weeks?

In the end, it was Laney who decided for us, waking from a bad dream and needing her mommy. I snuck out while Maeve was still up there, singing lullabies to Laney in a husky, loving voice. I left her a note saying I would call the next day and got in the truck smiling and sang along to my Patti Smith CD, loud, the whole way home. When I got there, the message light was blinking on my machine. It was Maeve.

She didn't say anything at all, just started in singing me a lullaby. "Too-ra-loo-ra-loo-ral, too-ra-loo-ra-li," she sang. I got ready for bed with her sweet, low voice echoing in my ears, glad again that we hadn't spent the night together this very first night. You've got to go slow, feeling your way, when you've got a time and materials job, otherwise you might miss something. I told her that the very first time I met her. There was nothing about Maeve I wanted to miss—not one thing—and I went off to sleep hoping that we'd be working together for a long, long time.

WHAT NO ONE ELSE HAS

Theda Hudson

The club was hopping. It could have had something to do with the program tonight, featuring *moi* as the demo sub.

Cass had me perched on a stool, showing off one of the newest corsets Bound for Fun offered.

I love corsets. I love the way they bind and shape. I love the way I feel when I wear them—super fem, super charged, ready for anything.

Cass says it's because I am—super fem, super charged, and ready for anything.

My smile widens at the thought of all these super-hot eyes on me.

One pair in particular. She's got beautiful tan skin, well-defined cheekbones, short spiky light brown hair, blatant, curious eyes (green like emeralds, twinkling in the soft overhead lights and softer ropes of lights strung along the tops of the walls), soft gray flannel slacks with a crease sharp enough to cut cheese, a button-down dove gray silky shirt with a charcoal tie, and a coarse-woven silvery jacket.

We've locked eyes a dozen times since I noticed her. I shift and arch my back, showing off my tits, which well up out of the tulip cups of the purple paisley velvet corset. I want to rub the black velvet trim at the top, but settle for shifting so it rubs itself along my full breasts.

Yeah, her pupils get bigger. I'm sure mine do. I know my smile does.

After the demo, my ass is red and my nipples are deliciously tender from Cass showing off the season's newest toys.

She's got another sub handling sales at the table while she sets up an open play session so we can show off more of the toys, encouraging more sales.

I catch the woman's eye again as she's refilling her glass at the refreshment bar. She smiles just a little. It's so delicious, I'm ambling over before I know what's what. I have to put together my own plate and water, so it's not like I don't have a reason to go, I tell myself when I'm nearly there.

My hips are really loose and I can feel my pussy buzz with pleasure and go all oozy at the thought of rubbing against those flannel pants.

I grab two bottles of water and then realize I still have to put together a plate for afterward. Stupid. She's watching me. And suddenly my body has lost the fluid grace I enjoy so much and I become spastic as I try to scoop fruit, crackers, and bread onto a paper plate.

There is no way I can carry everything and she knows it, too. "May I help?"

I turn and she's better looking even closer. Her skin is beautiful and I want to run a finger along her strong jaw, trace the line of her Cupid lips before planting my own right over them.

A small sigh escapes me. Her smile goes rakish. I bet she gets this reaction all the time.

I want to play with her. I want to bend over and stick my ass out so she can spank it. Her hand, a paddle, a moosehide flogger, I don't care. I want her hands, her mouth, and her eyes all over my tits.

I can smell my desire billowing up between us, mixing with the musky cologne she wears. She can smell me, too, and her eyebrow lifts in amusement.

"Please. Yes, please help me..." Help me come about a million times.

"Micky," she says, lifting the plate out of my hand, and her fingers, long and scrupulously manicured, touch mine. I flinch from the jolt I get. Not a shock, no, a connection.

I search her face, amazed by what just happened. She feels it, too, but she's calm under my gaze.

I swallow hard.

"I'm Lucy."

"I know," she says and I am flabbergasted for a moment. She knows my name!

"How, how did you know?"

She smiles patiently, like I'm an idiot. "Because they introduced you at the start of the program."

Stupid idiot, I thought.

"Of course."

"Where do you need to go?" she said magnanimously.

Right over your lap and never let me up.

"Over there," I said, pointing with one bottle at the Saint Andrew's cross.

She nodded. "After you."

I know I flushed, across my face, down my neck, and across my chest and back, when I realized she was going to watch me walk over there.

My hips, already loose, rolled and swayed and shimmied as I

made my way through the crowds to where Cass stood waiting for me.

I put the bottles on the console table where she had laid out the toys she wanted to demo.

"Here," I said to Micky.

She put the plate down.

"I hope you'll try out some of the toys," I said.

"No, I don't think so. I'll just watch."

All the air puffed out of me.

"Oh. Oh," I said like a complete bubblehead.

She smiled at bit at my flustered confusion.

Ah, just a little wicked. What, was she a voyeur? I could handle that.

I smirked.

"Thanks. I hope you enjoy the show."

She cocked her head and nodded, a sly smile creeping onto her face like a cat with an extra-nice bird in her mouth.

"Ready, Lucy?" Cass asked.

"Yes, sir," I said, dragging my eyes and head away from Micky's gaze.

She faded back behind the boundary circle Cass indicated, but I knew where she was.

Cass put the bunny fur cuffs on me. I twisted my wrists and legs around, as much to show them off as to feel the luxurious fur stroke my flesh.

"I'm going to use the latest in nipple clamps and weights," she says, showing off the anodized clamps and the different chain lengths.

I hate nipple clamps as much as I love pussy lip clamps.

Cass reaches into the corset and lifts my right breast out. Her hands are cold and I flinch a little as she tweaks my nipple to get it stand up.

As she attaches it, I soothe myself thinking of Micky's manicured fingers tightening the clamps, brushing across the tortured flesh, pulling at the chain that connects them. My pussy jerks and swells at the thought.

"We have a wide variety of weights in different themes. Each figure comes in a weight range and you can buys sets," Cass says. "Tonight only it's buy one, get one free." She hangs a sun, a crescent moon, and a starburst on the chain and smiles as I wince.

I look out over the crowd and catch sight of Micky. Her face is placid, but her eyes are locked onto me.

Cass gets the labial clamps set up, making lewd comments about the state of my arousal.

By the time she directs me to the cross and clips the cuffs to the eyebolts, I am buzzing high, touching the outer edges of subspace.

She demonstrates the various toys and oversees folks as they try them out on me. I'm a good one for this kind of demo. I can take a lot of mistakes and come out the other end just fine. I went into my head and took Micky with me.

Cass offered me water periodically and I drank greedily.

When it was over, she unclipped the clamps, rubbed my nipples as the blood flooded back in, and gave me a good long hit with the vibrator and a fat dildo to clench. After I came good and hard, she cleaned me up and helped me to the ratty green sofa and covered me with my favorite blue fleece blanket.

Several people came and thanked me for the exhibition. I kept watching for Micky, but she'd disappeared. I was disappointed. I hoped she'd come speak to me. A few women asked for my number. Those, I told to leave their names so I could check them out in time for the next party.

At last the crowd dissipated. I finished my snack and turned to putting lotion on my ass, thighs, and breasts.

As I pulled out my street clothes, Micky came back around and squatted down next to the couch.

"Very nice exhibit. You are quite beautiful in your distress, very graceful."

I swallowed. "Thank you."

"I'd like to see you. If you would be interested."

If I'd be interested.

"Tonight?"

She smiled regretfully.

"No, not tonight. May I have your number?"

I never gave my number out.

She saw my hesitation. "That's okay."

"No, no, please. I just..." What would I say? Protect myself from weirdos? That would be very good, Lucy.

I gave it to her.

She solemnly put it into her phone. "I'll be in touch."

I kept the phone on me for two weeks. Then I gave it up, thinking she'd lost interest, she thought I was a ditz for hesitating, she figured I'd given it to her to smooth over an awkward moment there and had no intention of seeing her.

I rethought the evening a hundred ways. I could have told her how interested I was. I could have begged her to have me, call me, whatever she wanted.

Just as all that faded away, she called.

"Lucy," she said when I answered. "It's Micky. Is now a good time to talk?"

"Yes, it is," I said stupidly, overjoyed to hear from her. She'd ask me to play. I could have her over. I got my own set of toys as part of my pay for doing the demos.

We made pleasantries for a few minutes and then she said, "*A Midsummer Night's Dream* is at the Buell. Would you like to go?"

Of all the things she could have asked, this was the last thing I would have thought of. Shakespeare? That was a torture I'd endured in high school.

It wasn't the kind of torture I envisioned as an adult.

I must have waited too long.

"Ah, the play's not the thing with you, is it?"

"No, no," I said, desperate to not miss out. "I mean, it's fine. I was, I was just distracted for a moment."

"Is this not a good time? I can call you again."

"No, no," I nearly shouted. "It's fine. I'd love to go. When?"

"I can get tickets for any time. We could have dinner before or after, whatever you like."

This was way stiffer than I imagined our first phone conversation to be. She was so polite, so thoughtful.

"Um, Friday?"

"This Friday? That's good. The show's at seven thirty. Do you want dinner before or after?"

"Uh, it'll have to be after. I don't get off until five thirty and I have to go home and dress."

Did I have anything suitable for a play? Micky was quite the dresser, so I'd need something nice.

"Good. That's fine. You just need to tell me where to pick you up."

Pick me up?

I must have paused too long again, because she said, "I can meet you downtown if you prefer. I understand."

"No, no." For Pete's sake, I'd just been thinking of having her over to play. What was wrong with me?

I gave her the address.

"Say six forty-five?"

"Okay."

I hung up and went directly to my closet to look for something to wear. Everything was either too casual or too slutty for a posh evening out.

I went shopping. I hated everything I tried on. I finally settled for a black gabardine pencil skirt and a short-waisted beaded matching jacket. My red satin corset would cover my tits, yet give me a suggestion of cleavage. And my grandmother's jet teardrop necklace would top it off.

She rang my bell, doorbell that is, promptly at six forty-five. I spritzed Poison in front of me and walked through the perfumy mist.

I must have looked all right because she just stood there for a long moment, drinking me in. I did my share of drinking, too, and I think we were both a little tipsy when I gestured her in. She wore a black, fitted suit with a snow white shirt that had gold-trimmed ebon button covers and a black silk bow tie. A red rose poked jauntily from her lapel. She carried a small box in one hand and lifted it with a flourish.

A corsage. I hadn't had one of those since senior prom. A beautiful blood-red bud nestled in a bed of baby's breath stared up at me.

"It's beautiful." I didn't know what to say. This was so different than what I wanted. Torture. That had to be it. Draw out the suspense. My teal silk panties got wet. They'd be sopping by the end of the night.

"Allow me," she said, taking the box from me. Our fingers touched and I felt the current even after that faint caress.

And it had been a caress.

She opened the box and lifted out the rose and two pins. Stepping in, she put the corsage to my left lapel and pinned it. I watched her concentrate as she maneuvered the pin through the cloth and the floral tape.

I wanted to kiss her, but settled for breathing in her scent. She wore the same cologne. I wished I had forgone my perfume so I could breathe her earthy, rich scent.

She stepped back.

"Very nice." She offered her arm and I grabbed my purse and keys from the table by the door.

I noticed as we walked that even with my fuck-me heels, she was still taller than me by a head.

We filled the drive downtown with inanities, tidbits about work, thoughts about dinner.

I just kept thinking about what would happen when she took me home. I'd laid out my favorite toys and several lengths of rope suitable for my four-poster bed.

She put me on her arm, and when we walked into the theater, our strides matched. I felt beautiful and proud to be by her side. We garnered our share of looks and she leaned over to whisper in my ear.

"Every man here wishes he was in my place."

Her breath warmed my neck and I felt the flush spread down my neck and across my back and chest. I smiled hugely.

The play was okay. I got the gist of it and laughed at most of the right places. I enjoyed it more than I thought I would, but all I wanted was to get her home.

When it was over and we were in the lobby, she asked, "Where would you like to have dinner? We can leave the car here and take a cab. I can't imagine you walking very far in those heels."

It was true. I had worn them because I know my calves look terrific in them. And the line when I bend over is stupendous, which is really where I wanted to be.

"Why don't we skip dinner and go back to my place?"

Her face froze for a moment and then became regretful. I had said the wrong thing. But why?

"I'd prefer not to."

Irritation rose up.

"Why not? The connection is there. We both felt it, didn't we?"

She nodded. "Oh, yes. It's there."

"Then why? Do you just want an arm toy?" A sneaking suspicion rose up. She watched, she teased, and watched some more.

"Are you some kind of pervert? Do you get off watching because you can't do anything else?" I realized I was getting loud and lowered my voice.

Her face froze again and she just stared at me.

Finally, she shook her head. "No, Lucy, I'm as red-blooded as you."

"Then what is it? You want me, I want you, what is stopping you?"

She smiled sadly. "Yes, I want you. But everyone wants you. Everyone has you."

Everyone has me? I'd never felt ashamed of my popularity or my desire or my reputation as a play slut before. But that comment made me feel dirty, like a whore. I flushed, humiliated and ashamed.

"Now, I've done it. I didn't mean to insult you. I meant that I want what no one else has."

"And what's that?" I growled, tears of anger and shame filling my eyes.

"Your heart. I want to woo you," she said softly.

Oh. Now I was really embarrassed. Here she was *courting* me, and I had been stupid. Really stupid. Ruined everything.

"No one ever did that before."

She smiled sadly. "No," she said softly. "But you deserve it. Perhaps I should take you home."

I blushed again and tears dripped down my cheeks, streaking my mascara. She handed me a handkerchief. A handkerchief!

I took it and blotted my eyes, unwilling, unable to look at her.

She took my arm and we walked silently to the car. I got in when she opened it and sat, smelling her cologne as she walked around to the driver's side and let herself in.

We said nothing all the way home.

When she pulled up in front of my house, she got out and opened the door. I got out, taking her hand, but not feeling any of the electricity we'd shared before. Because I broke the connection. Because I was a dumb broad who couldn't recognize class and gallantry when it took my arm.

"Here," she said, offering me a card. "Call me if you feel like it."

I tucked the card in my purse as a fresh wave of hot tears flowed down my cheeks. I couldn't look at her as I walked up the steps to my door.

She waited until I was in before driving away.

Once in, I threw my purse down on the side table and kicked off my shoes.

"Stupid, stupid, Lucy," I shouted, tugging off the jacket and unlacing the corset. My toys were all spread out on their towel on the bed and I flipped the corner, sending them flying hard into the wall.

I sat on the bed, weeping from anger at myself, shame at what I'd thought and said, and regret over what I had lost.

I got into the shower and ran it until it was cold and my tears ran dry. Then I dried off and crawled into bed, miserable.

It was a week before I could think about what she'd said. Then I remembered she'd given me her card. I found it and stared at it. I couldn't possibly call her. I was too humiliated.

On the other hand, she hadn't said she didn't want to see me again. I would have. I'd have thought I was too dumb to woo. Not worthy of such affection.

Those thoughts haunted me for another week.

Then I saw *Man of La Mancha* was coming to the Arvada Center. I loved that movie.

I handled the card so much the edges got worn and I finally decided that I'd better call before there were no more tickets or I couldn't read the card anymore.

She picked up on the first ring. "This is Micky."

"This is Lucy," I said, my voice cracking.

"Lucy," she said, real warmth coloring my name. "How are you?"

She never said, it took you long enough, I thought you'd never call. No, she was going to make this easy.

If only I could make the most of it without being a twit.

"I, I've thought a lot about what you said. I owe you an apology. I, no one's ever courted me before." I swallowed. I had to be honest here. "It's embarrassing, but all I thought about was getting you alone and playing."

She laughed, a throaty chuckle. "I admit I've thought about it a lot, too."

She had?

"But then why..."

"Because, Lucy, like I said, I want your heart. Everything else will follow after that."

It would?

I could hardly breathe. She wanted my heart. She still wanted it, even after what I did.

"Uh. Well, I called to say that *Man of La Mancha* is playing at the Arvada Center."

She didn't say anything for a long moment.

"You know that I chose *Midsummer Night's Dream* for a reason, don't you?"

She had? I thought frantically. A romantic comedy, star-crossed love, mix-ups. How did that relate?

"Uh, no."

"So then you aren't trying to say something to me?"

Don Quixote tilting at windmills, chasing dreams that could never be realized.

"Gawd, I am such a doofus." If my face was any redder, it would spontaneously combust. I was glad she couldn't see it.

She laughed again, that same throaty chuckle. It sent shivers down my back and lodged in my pussy.

"Well, I could have given a clue, I guess."

Maybe a couple. On the other hand, I was in a groove all my own.

"No, I just loved the movie and thought it would be fun to see it in the flesh."

"Good enough," she said. "When do you want to go?"

Now, right now. Wait. I'd need a new outfit.

"Saturday night?" I asked.

"Dinner first?"

Be decisive.

"At the Palomino Club?"

"Great," Micky said. "I'll pick you up at five."

I hoped my voice didn't show how my hands were shaking.

"Until five, then."

Well, it quavered a little.

"Good-bye, Lucy," she said.

"Good-bye, Micky," I said.

My dress for Saturday was a purple floral satin brocade sheath with matching pumps and a black pashmina scarf.

Her eyes lit up like Christmas lights when I opened the door.

She wore a dark blue suit with a cream button-down shirt and a narrow navy and cream tie.

She had another corsage, a wristlet this time.

How did she know which to bring? I don't know, but I didn't doubt she could do it again and again.

I had my little perk, too. When we sat down to dinner, I pulled a slim lavender envelope out of my purse.

She held it up and inspected it. I'd made the paper a year ago, but never knew what to do with it. I made the lacy edging with a pair of fancy scissors. She held it to her nose and closed her eyes as she inhaled.

"Poison," she said. "I love what it does for you."

She noticed what the perfume did for me? I flushed. I was such a fool. But a lucky one.

She opened it carefully and withdrew another small piece of handmade paper that I'd spent all of yesterday making. It took three tries to get the color and the consistency the way I wanted it.

Her eyes grew shiny as she held up the dainty blood-red heart with "Lucy" written in my most ornate hand across the center.

"Not to hurry things along or anything."

"Liar," she said.

"Okay, maybe a little, but I mean it."

She stared at me, her face serious, her eyes wondering, seriously wondering.

"Oh, Micky," I said. "I don't deserve you, not yet, but I will, I swear I will."

"Thank you, Lucy." Her eyes were the tiniest bit shiny as she brought the heart to her lips and kissed it before tucking it gently into her inside breast pocket.

She lifted my hand and turned it over to kiss my palm. A thrill shot up my arm, straight to my heart.

Dinner was wonderful, the musical a treat I will never forget, tons better live than the movie ever was, and, yes, Micky pulled me inside when I opened the door to my house, took me in her arms, and kissed me full on the mouth.

We never even opened the toy bag, but now that we know each other so well, I bet that she'll use them.

A lot.

But just on me.

A PROM STORY IN THREE PARTS

Sheree L. Greer

I.

I had walked in on my mother and father. They were just talking, but the fact that I had never met Ray, my absentee father of seventeen years, made the moment as salacious as me walking in on something else. Of course I stormed out. I went to Daryan's. Tentative and tender, she sat on the floor of her room and held my hand while I slept in her bed. A friend was what I needed, and that is what Daryan gave me, friendship. I went through the weeks leading up to prom terse and tense, unsure how to proceed. My mother had apologized and hugged me. I had kept my arms at my side. We didn't see each other much with her working overtime, and it was just as well. I didn't want to see her. I didn't want to talk to her. All of that changed the night of prom.

"Zaire, come in my room a minute."

I left the bathroom, where I was finishing my eye makeup, and went into my mother's room. I sat down on the bed. I wore a silver gown that complemented my gray eyes. I scratched the back of my neck nervously, my hair done up in an elegant French roll, and watched as my mother went into one of her jewelry boxes. She took out a small black box lined with silver. She held it out to me.

"What is it?" I asked with a sigh.

"I know you're still upset with me, but you need to let me explain." She jutted the box toward me. "Here. Take it. I want you to wear these tonight."

I opened the small velveteen box. Inside, resting regally on a small hump of black satin, was a pair of diamond earrings. I held them up, astounded. The light hit the pea-sized stones and came exploding out in twinkles of purple, blue, pink, yellow, and white.

"They're beautiful," I said.

"So are you," my mother said.

I closed the box and held it, biting the inside of my jaw.

"Zaire, I should've handled the situation with Ray better. He'd been calling me, saying he was moving back to Milwaukee and wanted to know if I'd forgiven him. He asked about you and Sierra. And the other night, I let him stop by. It was only supposed to be for a minute. He said he's changed. He's ready to be a family, wants to be a father to you and Sierra, to his 'baby girls,' he said."

"Does he even know how old we are? Baby girls? I'm graduating from high school in a few weeks. Sierra's in eighth grade. He's awfully damn late."

"Watch your mouth, Zaire." My mother rubbed her hands. "I know. I know. That's what we were arguing about. He's said these things before, about changing. And in the end, I always end up hurt and disappointed. I don't want that for you and Sierra. I don't want you hurt or disappointed by Ray the way I've been."

Protecting us. She was trying to protect us. My eyes watered.

"You should've said something," I said.

"I know. But I didn't know what to say. I wasn't sure what to make of any of it. I'm sorry. It wasn't a good secret to keep. Talking it out might've even helped." My mother sighed.

I instantly thought of my dreams. I did my best to ignore them, shamefully shutting them out of my everyday life, trying to forget them the second I woke up. The dreams were more vivid each time. What had started as a soft presence, a closeness warming behind me, faceless and gentle, breath against my neck, skin like silk at my back, had become something infinitely more detailed, more telling.

Daryan, a transfer student new to Adams High, had invaded my dreams the moment I met her. In the dream, we are both naked. Daryan is behind me. I feel her nipples grazing my shoulder blades as she inhales, and when she exhales, a sweet sigh escaping her throat. I feel her breath, hot and urgent, against the back of my neck. When I turn to face her, she smiles a smile I've given a thousand meanings—amusement, compassion, intrigue, invitation. I smile, too, and feel weightless. Daryan places her warm, soft hands on my shoulders and her touch becomes the only thing that keeps me from floating away.

I awake to the sound of my own gasp, wrapped in the darkness of my bedroom. The quiet black is my only solitude and it gives me a solace the slickness between my legs won't allow. I place my hand there, across the lips that thankfully never speak, and stifle feelings I pray are the kind that remain hidden and not the ones that cannot be denied. Afraid and trembling with shame, I clench my eyes tight and pray myself back to sleep.

"Say something," my mother said. She put her hand on my thigh.

"I guess I can understand that."

My mother slid the jewelry box from my hands and opened it. "Ray bought these for me. Right before I got pregnant with Sierra." She took one of the impressive studs out of the box and twirled it between her thumb and forefinger. "Come here."

I sniffled and leaned toward her. She put the earring in my ear and rubbed my lobe.

"Then, a week later, he came over to Mama Iris's, where we staying, and asked me to give them back to him."

"What? Why?" I turned so she could put the other earring on. She placed it just so, then held my face in her hands.

"He had lost a pool game. Bet more than he had, owed some man a few hundred dollars more. I refused. He clenched his fist like he was going to hit me. I clenched mine, too. You came running up to the door. He looked at you, then looked at me, cursed, and left. It was the last time I had seen him. Last time you seen him, too."

"Until the other night." I didn't remember ever seeing Ray at all. I imagined myself, at four years old, running up to the door to kick him in the shins.

"Yeah." My mother kissed my forehead. "You sure are beautiful, Zaire. You're beautiful and caring. And good. You're really good. I don't want anyone to spoil that, especially not your father."

She took me in her arms. I lifted my arms around her, clinging to her while fighting tears. The moment made me feel sad and a little guilty. There I was condemning her for not telling me the whole story, all the while clutching secrets of my own.

My boyfriend Sheldon arrived at 7:30 sharp, looking like a male model in a black tuxedo with crisp white shirt and perfectly matched gray vest and bow tie. He wore black square-toe shoes and had a diamond stud of his own shining in his right ear.

He smiled broadly when he saw me, his dimples deeper than I had seen them in a while.

"You look absolutely amazing," he said. He held out my corsage, a delicate white lily with baby's breath and pink miniature roses.

"Thank you," I said. "You look nice, too."

He adjusted the flowers on my wrist and put an arm around me. He seemed tense, his body a little stiff and awkward.

"I don't know why I'm nervous," he whispered to me as my mother scurried around trying to find the best place for us to pose for pictures.

She took several shots of us in front of the fireplace and a few more when we got outside. My younger sister Sierra squealed and Mama Iris, my grandmother, grinned with each new picture while my mother kept wiping her eyes and shaking her head in awe and pride.

"Y'all look fantastic together," my mother said. "Let me get one more."

She took five more.

Sheldon looked at his watch.

"We gotta go, Mama," I said.

"All right, all right," my mother said. "One more." She snapped another picture, then motioned for Sheldon to go on ahead to the car.

"I want you to be happy. Above all else. You know that, don't you?" my mother said.

I nodded, and my mother kissed my cheeks. We hugged. I blew Sierra, Mama Iris, and my mother kisses as Sheldon backed out of the driveway.

II.

Prom, "This Night Forever," was at the Winchester Hotel down-town. I had never been there, but from the looks of the tall glass building with gold-detailed doors and elegant spotlights, I knew it was going to be something special inside.

Limos pulled up and drove off after dropping off beaming teenagers in a wide array of backless, strapless, and flowing gowns paired with sharp, tailored tuxes and fine suits. A few people came in with Sheldon and me, having left borrowed and rented luxury sedans in the care of the valet.

Once inside, it wasn't hard to find the ballroom. Though a placard on an easel welcomed the John Adams High School Senior Prom in an elegant script of embossed gold letters, you could hear the music spilling into the spacious lobby.

Inside the ballroom, a hip-hop classic, Naughty by Nature's "Hip Hop Hooray" blared from the giant speakers on either side of the DJ booth. There was a long table with fruit and cheese trays surrounding a block of ice sculpted into a towering ninety-eight. The ballroom was packed. There were three strobe lights and two enormous disco balls. A smoke machine puffed from behind one of the speakers and blue, yellow, green, and red beams of light shot up and out from beneath the DJ's table.

Sheldon held my hand and I waved to a few classmates, said a few hellos, and exchanged dress admiration with some girls from my homeroom as their dates stood quiet and nervous behind them.

"Zaire, I'm so glad you're here!" My friend Jamia threw her arms around me. "I need you."

"What's going on?" I asked. "You look great! The dress turned out wonderfully."

Jamia did a quick spin and halfhearted curtsy. Her dress was baby blue with an intricate web of white lace across the strapless bodice. It wrapped around her thick hips and thighs and cascaded to the floor, ending in a lace hem that dovetailed into a train behind her.

"You look good, too. That dress is gorgeous. And your date ain't half-bad either." She nudged Sheldon. He smiled.

"Well, what's the problem? Where's Creisha?" I looked for our third musketeer.

"Exactly." Jamia grabbed my arm. "Sheldon, you'll have to excuse us."

Jamia pulled me toward the side door of the ballroom and yanked me through the heavy doors into a bare hallway glowing with orange overhead lights. We stood in the hallway and met Creisha, who was leaning against the wall, her tiny brown purse on the floor next to her shoes, sexy little brown strappy stilettos.

"Hey," I said. "What's wrong?"

"Three hoes in there got on my dress! That's what's wrong."

Her dress was nice. It was chocolate brown with one strap over her left shoulder and tiny swirls of velvet-like material all over the satin dress.

"Who knew anyone would wear brown to prom?" Jamia shook her head.

"That's what the hell I thought." Creisha was heated. She kicked one of her shoes. "This is some bullshit."

"Well, you can't stay in this hallway all night," I said. I picked up her shoe and held it out to her.

"I know. I know. But I don't want to be out there with three damn clones out there with me." Creisha put her shoes on.

"Look, it happens. But it's not the end of the world. It's all about who's wearing it best. And I can bet you that you look better in this dress than any of those other girls." I put my arm around Creisha. She stiffened, then relaxed.

"You're right. I'm being dramatic."

"Understatement of the year," Jamia said.

"Shut up." Creisha cut her eyes at her. "Not everybody can get a specially made dress around here."

Jamia shrugged.

"Let's go show everyone who's wearing the dress best." I smiled and rubbed Creisha's back.

"Yeah. Let's go." Creisha put her arm around my waist, Jamia pulled the door open, and the three of us walked back into the ballroom.

The music was great. I danced with Sheldon for a few songs, and when he got tired, I danced with some other people from school, even dancing by myself for four songs in a row.

"Top of the World" came on and couples converged, dancing close, cheek to cheek or heads resting on shoulders. I started looking for Sheldon but stopped when I heard someone call my name. I turned toward the ice sculpture. The nine-eight had melted down, and it looked like Stonehenge, the image indiscernible blocks open for interpretation.

Daryan stood behind the table. I went toward her and she met me halfway. My heart burst at the sight of her, the pieces trickling down my insides like sparks from fireworks falling into Lake Michigan.

Daryan wore a flowing white strapless dress. Her breasts were full, swelling from the beaded bodice. The dress looked creamy, like a waterfall of sweet coconut milk against her dark skin. Her dreads were pinned back into a ball; her eyes and expression were sharp. Her beauty cut me, sliced me right down the middle. Splayed, I felt exposed.

"Damn," I said.

"Damn yourself." Daryan stepped closer to me, and I took

another step toward her. We embraced tentatively, as if we didn't want to touch each other, but the very opposite was true.

"You look…you…you're…" I was stammering. "I didn't…I didn't think you were coming."

"It's senior prom." Daryan grinned. "Nine-eight and all that." She pumped her arms, raising the roof with a roll of her eyes. "It's part of the whole experience, right?"

I smiled and nervously rubbed the back of my neck.

"You having a good time?" she asked.

"Um, yeah," I said. "I've been dancing and…"

"Where's your people? Jamia and Creisha…and I imagine Sheldon's here, too."

"Oh, they're around." I shrugged and waved my hand toward the dance floor. "You came alone?"

Daryan nodded.

I shook my head. It seemed a shame, a pure injustice that someone so beautiful would ever be anywhere alone. I was about to invite her to walk around with me when Jamia and Creisha came running up to us.

"Oh my God, Daryan. Girl, you look good," Creisha said.

Jamia, stunned, finally found her voice. "You look great!"

"Thank you." Daryan looked at me, and I looked away.

"You here with somebody?" Creisha asked, feeling the material of Daryan's dress.

"Nope," Daryan said. "I just came to check it out."

"You doing more than checking it out looking like this." Creisha walked around Daryan, sizing her up. "I didn't know you had a body like that either," she said, slapping Daryan's ass.

"Well, you know, I couldn't show up in jeans." Daryan shrugged and smoothed the front of her dress. We all shared a laugh.

"Anyway, Zaire, we were coming to find you because

Sheldon was looking for you. Plus, we getting ready to go," Creisha said.

"Where y'all going?" I asked.

"We're not leaving together, dummy," Creisha said. "We just happen to be leaving at the same time. I think Sheldon's ready to go, too."

Jamia sighed. "It's getting boring. I'm about to grab my date and leave. We're going to get something to eat and then I'm going home. This one here," she jabbed her thumb at Creisha, "is going to the Hilton with Greg."

"The Hilton?" Daryan said. "Nice."

Creisha smirked. "Yeah. The Hilton. It's a special night, right?"

"That's what I hear," Daryan said. She looked into my eyes. I looked away, contemplating the thinning dance floor.

"Guess I'll see you all next week. I know there'll be plenty of stories to tell." Jamia gave each of us a hug and a kiss on the cheek. Even Daryan. The gesture surprised her. It showed on her face. Jamia and Creisha had been distant with Daryan since rumors of her being a dyke began rippling throughout Adams High.

"Have a good night. I know I will," Creisha said. She followed Jamia's lead, but gave out one-armed hugs and air kisses.

Daryan and I were left alone.

"So you're about to go?" she asked.

"Yeah. I should. I mean, Sheldon's looking for me and..."

"It's cool. I just came to show my face. And to see you." Daryan looked down at the floor, then up at me.

My face flushed.

"You really look amazing, Zaire." Daryan smiled and hugged me. She kissed my cheek. My body went rigid. Her lips were as soft as they looked.

"Give me a call tomorrow," she said.

"Okay," I said. "I will."

Daryan turned and walked out of the ballroom. I watched her until I couldn't see her anymore.

III.

After we left the Winchester, Sheldon took me to Konos. Even though I had been the one doing all the dancing, he proclaimed several times on the way to the Greek restaurant that he was starving. He inhaled a cheese steak and side of fries as I picked at a Reuben. I didn't even know why I ordered anything. I wasn't hungry, just tired and ready to go home. Seeing Daryan had done something to me, made me retreat into myself, wanting nothing more than to be left alone.

Once in the car, Sheldon put his hand on my thigh as he drove. I thought for sure he was taking me home. I had told him while we were at the restaurant that my mother didn't want me out all night.

"She gave you a curfew tonight? Tonight? Prom night?" he had said incredulously. "That's some bullshit."

I told him that she wanted me home by three a.m. It was two when he pulled up to Dineen Park. He parked, and we got out. We walked over to the man-made pond and sat down on the steps. I shivered and Sheldon put his jacket around my shoulders.

"I got us a room," he said.

"Oh," I said. We were looking out at the water. It was like staring out at a pool of ink, the water still and black, seeming thick and substantial. "I'm sorry. I should have told you I'd have a curfew."

"It's all right." Sheldon put his arm around me. "What can you do? You could bust it, but…" He raised an eyebrow. I twisted my lips. "Right, right. Anyway, I had a good time tonight. I enjoyed you." He kissed my cheek.

"Me, too." A small family of ducks rearranged themselves in front of us. The water gurgled and splashed. The ducks quacked and fluttered.

"Really? I kind of felt like you were avoiding me or something."

"Why did you think that?"

"You seem distant. Like you want to be somewhere else. With someone else."

"What?" I shook my head. "No. No, I just have a lot on my mind."

"Like what?"

"I don't want to talk about it."

"You regret it don't you? You wish we never had sex."

I gasped. Having sex with Sheldon was a test. I needed answers, and sleeping with him in the cool damp of his mother's basement was the only way to combat the dead end the library had been. When I dreamt about Daryan, I started researching. I found books on the sexual revolution of the 1960s, Stonewall and Daughters of Bilitis. Feminisim. Lesbian rights movements, MtF, FtM, PFLAG, HRC, and GLBT. But everything I found was all too far away. Too formal, too removed. Where were the stories about young women like me, faced with the questions I had, the fears that had been multiplying like gremlins in the pit of my stomach? I had gathered my courage, attempted to face it somehow, to figure something out, and come up with nothing. There was nothing. Nothing about dreams, desires, demanding mothers, and disconcerting best friends. There was nothing like me, nothing like Daryan. Maybe it was all an apparition. I was being haunted and there was nothing really there. Testing myself with Sheldon felt like all I could do.

"So, you gonna say something or..."

"Sheldon, I don't want to talk about it right now. Can you just take me home?" I asked, looking at him and clutching his jacket under my neck.

"Fine," he said. "Let's go."

Sheldon walked me to the door. He pulled me into him, holding me close.

"We're going to have to talk about us soon, Zaire," Sheldon said.

"I'll call you tomorrow." A lump formed in my throat. A million things I needed to say lodged in my throat like a rock. I kissed him lightly, feeling like saying good-bye and meaning it in every sense of the word.

The house was dark and quiet when I stepped inside. I slipped out of my shoes so they wouldn't clack against the hardwood floors. I snuck downstairs and grabbed a pair of sneakers. I snatched the car keys off the hook in the kitchen and quietly pulled the front door closed as I left.

When I got to Daryan's house, I tossed tiny pebbles up at her dark windows. Just before I was about to give up, the square window on the side of the house went from black to yellow. The shade lifted and Daryan looked down, her dreads wild.

"What are you doing here?" she asked when she came down to open the door.

"I'm not sure." I took a deep breath.

"Come on," she said. She opened the door to the apartment and I stepped inside. I still had on Sheldon's jacket over my dress. With my stockings and black Reeboks, I knew I looked ridiculous.

Daryan stood before me with her hands on her hips. She had on a pair of gray jogging pants, baggy and hanging off her hips, with a tight white tank top that stopped at her navel. Her belly button was deep, and I found myself staring at it, imagining myself diving into it. Diving into her.

"What's going on, Zaire?" Daryan looked concerned and serious.

"I had to see you," I said. "I've been thinking about a lot of stuff, trying to figure shit out and..." My voice was breaking as I spoke. Tears sprang to my eyes. I wiped them and looked away.

Daryan grabbed my hand. "Let me show you something."

"Okay."

Daryan led me into her bedroom. She ushered me next to the bed, then went over to the bookshelf. She stretched behind the tower of books, and her arm finally emerged with a rolled canvas. She unfurled the canvas and spread it as best she could across the bed.

It was a painting. Two hands reaching toward each other. Strong, black hands with slender fingers and incredible detail, veins and creases, cuticles and perfect nails. One reaching outward, a finger slightly extended, like pointing but more like reaching out, intending to touch. The other hand was relaxed in its reach, but still wanting, moving toward the extended finger.

It was familiar. I had seen the two hands once before but couldn't place it. The background of the painting was grayish blue with carefully placed hairline cracks that gave the painting a look of historic beauty, the almost-touching hands a message painted across ancient marble.

"It's called *God's Finger*. My father painted it," Daryan said. "It's from the creation story on the ceiling of the Sistine Chapel. My father did a close-up of the hands, God's and Adam's, from heaven to Earth." She pointed at the canvas.

I stood back. "It's beautiful."

"Yeah, it's my favorite one. He made the hands so elegant

and delicate. They seem warm, promising. Safe." Daryan lifted the canvas and held it up.

"They look like women's hands," I said.

Daryan looked at me and back at the painting. She stretched it back out on the bed and we stood shoulder to shoulder, each holding a corner.

"They do. They do look like women's hands," she said with a laugh.

"Aren't they supposed to touch? The fingers touch in the real painting, don't they? God's finger and Adam's hand?"

"No." Daryan smiled. "They don't touch."

"I don't know why I always think of them that way. The hands touching."

"Because you want them to...to touch, to make contact. Create sparks." She winked at me.

Daryan moved closer to me. Our shoulders touched, then our pinky fingers. She moved her hand on top of mine and looked at me.

I met her eyes and moved my face toward hers. Daryan hesitated, then leaned in. Our mouths came together in slow motion, the gentleness of the kiss like a blessing, the warmth of her mouth like coming home.

Daryan pulled away, and I opened my eyes. She let go of her end of the canvas. It slowly began curling closed. The roll met my hand, and I eased off the painting, letting the curl complete itself. Daryan reached over, grabbed the painting, and placed it on the floor beside the bed.

We stood facing each other. Daryan moved slowly, like she was underwater, her hands pushing the tuxedo jacket off my shoulders. My chest heaved and my body tingled with a charge I'd never felt before, not for real, not in waking life. She closed the space between us with one step. She slid a single finger across my collarbone, hooking the spaghetti strap of my dress and pulling it off my shoulder. She tilted her head as she leaned toward me, her lips parting. I felt her breath on my skin. It was warm and cool at the same time, sweet and sharp like peppermint. She pressed her mouth against my shoulder. Daryan. My dream. My reality.

Moving her lips from my shoulder, she faced me, and her eyes cut to the very core of me. The sharpness of her beauty split me in two. Our lips met again, and she filled the space between my two selves. Her mouth, her breath, making me whole.

"You're shaking. Are you scared?" Daryan asked in a husky whisper. "If you're scared, we don't have to do anything. I don't want you to be scared."

"I'm...not...scared," I said, barely choking out the words.

Daryan lifted up my left arm. She held it up, and we both watched my hand quake. She raised her scarred eyebrow.

"That's not because I'm afraid," I said. My words came out steady and strong, certain and true. Though light-headed and woozy from Daryan's kisses, I stood firmly on my feet, the wetness between my legs serving as an anchor, my body heavy with want.

"Well, what is it?"

"I'm shaking because I've never wanted to touch anyone so bad in my entire life."

Daryan pulled me toward her and kissed me hard and deep. She slid the other strap from my shoulder and slowly turned me around. She moved slowly, cautiously, like everything about me was fragile, new.

I turned to face her. I stepped out of my underwear. I stood before her naked. My breath slow and deep, my hands shaking, I gripped the bottom of her shirt and lifted it up. She raised her arms and I pulled her shirt up over her head. Her dreads settled themselves as she slid the tank top off her long arms. I looked at Daryan, her eyes, her mouth, her chin, neck, shoulders, and arms. I put my hands on her shoulders and ran my fingers down her arms, across her stomach, and up to her chest. Her deep brown skin was soft, beautiful, and comforting. She was an African violet and I wanted to be her water.

"You're absolutely sure?" she asked, holding my hands.

"Yes."

"How do you know?" She touched my face.

Dreaming was something I had been doing for far too long. I had been running on raw emotion since sitting at Dineen Park with Sheldon. In that moment, I had closed my eyes as the ducks shifted, making quiet splashes and ripples in the pond. The scene was serene, beautiful, sweet. When I opened my eyes, I had wished for magic. I wished for Daryan. Beside me. I wanted her beside me. Always.

"I know because being here with you is all I want. It's all I've ever wanted."

There were no more words. Our lips came together, and the world shifted. No longer heavy and weighed down, I became weightless, losing myself in the sensation of Daryan's smooth, naked body against mine. We were on her bed, fitting together in ways I had never imagined. Daryan pushed her hips against my hips, pulling me closer and closer, holding me tighter and tighter as we moved gracefully beside, underneath, and on top of each other.

The heat between my legs grew unbearable. My head lolled back as Daryan licked my hipbones and massaged my thighs.

When her lips and tongue finally met the throbbing ache between my legs, I wanted to sing. The pleasure that I had always kept hidden, a tiny contentment, an eternal secret tucked deep inside myself, grew into something bigger, louder, and more powerful than I thought possible. It rushed over me in great oceanic waves, lifting me up, higher and higher and higher, carrying me away into the seductive expanse of the mysterious, the magical, and the unknown.

MISTY AND ME

by Catherine Paulssen

I was a cliché.

Falling in love with my best friend—can that happen outside of Hollywood?

Fools rush in, they say.

Sometimes, fools tumble slowly.

Being in love with your best friend. It can be the best thing that ever happened to you. It can be the worst. In my case, it must be the latter. I wrapped my jacket tighter around myself and scowled at the glum beach underneath a cloudy sky.

A golden retriever, far ahead of its owner, came romping around me, wagging its tail. McAllister's dog. I stroked its damp fur and furiously blinked the tears away.

My best friend. It wasn't the boy I had built castles in the sand with when we were kids, living next door to each other.

It was Misty.

Misty, who would watch people on the bus and invent stories in her head about where they came from and what they were up to. Who could crease her mouth into a smile so broad that her eyes, heavy-lidded gray eyes, would become small underneath her ginger fringes. Misty, who would never miss a Robert Mitchum movie being rerun on TV, and who was freaked out by ants.

I knew the lilt of her voice when she was lying about how she really felt, and I knew the moment she would come out of that hiding place deep inside her to confess, to cry or rant. I knew how she tried to be the best mom to her son, and how she struggled every day with the notion of having failed him. In moments like these, I would hug her and tell her that she was the bravest person I had ever known. I would hold her until the tension left her body.

Lately, a new feeling had sneaked its way into the safety that was our embrace. Her curvaceous body pressed against mine filled me with anxiety, with desire, with shame. I wanted to bury my face in the crook of her neck, vanish in her smell that reminded me of the skin of fresh apples which had been lying in the sun, and I knew it would take away my ability to breathe. Everything within me started to hum, my skin was getting heated and flushed, my palms became sweaty. I would watch my hands behind her back, lying on the small of her back, the tips of my fingers tingling with the wish to trace the curve of her neck.

I smothered the sensations as soon as they started to crawl up inside me, shame following in their wake. I was betraying our friendship, a friendship tried and tested since I had moved to the small town on the northern coast. I wasn't sure if I would be able to remain quiet about it, or how long it would take before my guilty conscience would scream out and beg for forgiveness. The fear of that moment, and even more of what would follow it, scared me.

But what scared me most was that from the way she said my

name when her guard was down I could tell she felt it too.

Our first kiss was a cliché.

Sitting next to her in the only movie theater within a fifty-mile radius, the tactic with which the hero would conquer his lady obvious after the first twenty minutes, I tried to make out her profile in the semidarkness: the small button nose that made her look younger than she was, the protruding eyes reflecting the picture on the screen, the thick strands falling over her forehead. Lost in the sight of her, I didn't even notice I was staring until she turned. For a few moments, she just looked at me, her expression unreadable in the shadows that covered her eyes, now that she had averted them from the screen. Then, suddenly, her teeth shimmered in the dim room. She was smiling her big-mouthed smile. And it was shining on me.

I'm sure I smiled back. I must have. Or maybe I didn't.

I will never know.

What I do know is the feeling of her fingers around mine as she took my hand, her cool, short digits around my long, warm ones. Holding them tight. I lowered my eyes and watched the small marvel that our clasped hands were. When I raised them again, Misty was still looking at me. I tried to figure out what her face was telling me, and saw confusion, shyness. But at the same time, tenderness. And confidence.

Her lips came closer as I tilted my head. She was sharing my breath now. I could feel the heat of her mouth. Her eyes still held me captive, her breath, quickened, smelled of chocolate and popcorn. It brushed my lips. Misty riveted her attention on my lips, and I closed my eyes.

And then she kissed me. Shyly, her mouth pressed on mine. I parted my lips, only a bit, but as if she had waited for a cue, her lips seized mine more boldly.

I'm not sure what caused it—the darkness, the triumphant music in the background indicating the movie was reaching a romantic peak, or Misty's determination—but my inhibitions evaporated. I prodded her lips with my tongue, and she opened hers.

In an attempt to draw her further into our kiss, I raised my fingers and ran them through her short hair. I couldn't remember being kissed like that. Or having kissed someone like I kissed Misty that night. As our lips broke apart, she opened her eyes, her stare meeting mine.

I cupped her face and brushed her cheek with my thumb. And there it was again—the feeling of anxiety. Only this time, it remained a short notion that was suppressed by instant, delirious giddiness. Misty searched my face and slid her arm around me. I leaned my head against her shoulder and stared into the dim cinema, not seeing anything of what was happening onscreen.

She stroked my fingers. "Jules," she whispered.

It was all she said.

Our first night was a cliché.

We let the others leave the room until all the rows were empty and end credits faded out before we left the theater in silence, like young lovers who don't want to be confronted by anything that reminds them there's a real world outside.

Besides, even in our state of bliss we knew that if we were seen on the main street holding hands, by this time tomorrow, the whole town would know.

With her son gone to stay at a friend's for the night, her house lay dark and silent in between the conifers, like a refuge to our newfound secret. Misty closed the door behind us and gave me one of the long looks I had seen a lot lately. "Want to go upstairs?"

I nodded.

She let me go ahead and waited until I sat down on her bed. Her eyes wandered over my face as she brushed some strands of hair behind my ear. I leaned back into her pillows.

She turned her eyes to the ribbons of my vintage empire blouse and tentatively tugged at one band's end. The bow came apart. I watched her fingers loosening the second ribbon. She didn't look up but kept her gaze fixed on the blouse's opening coming apart. She placed her cool hand at the small spot of skin revealed and parted the fabric. I was certain I had stopped breathing some minutes ago, but my heaving breast said otherwise. One by one, she opened the small buttons below the ribbons. When the blouse was open, Misty looked up. Her gray eyes were dark.

We didn't say a word.

I stroked her hand and drew her close for a kiss. A smile flashed over her face, then her eyes traveled back to my chest. Cautiously, she tugged the blouse away to reveal my white mesh bra underneath. I noticed how I was neither embarrassed at wearing my most boring bra nor shy about what she might think of my less-than-perfect figure.

"Beautiful," she whispered, and started to move her finger along the bra's outline.

I tried to anticipate her next move, wanting her to undress me completely, but Misty didn't sense my silent urging, or didn't want to. She watched the sight of me; the blouse completely open now, she took it all in: my pale skin, my small breasts, the little mole above my navel. Very slowly, she bent over me and started to place small kisses on the line between my breasts.

I propped myself up on my elbows so she could open the bra, and shivered when she finally did. She covered my right breast with her hand and cupped it very gently, as if she was holding a delicate treasure. I stared at her hand, and the thrill that rushed

over me when her thumb finally started to move over my nipple...
I gnawed my lips to bite back the groan building in my throat.

Teasingly, tenderly, she traced my left breast's shape, drawing smaller and smaller circles around the nipple, and when I was convinced my senses couldn't be sharpened any further, she enclosed the nipple with her lips and gently sucked on it. I could hear myself moaning as I closed my eyes and pushed my head back.

She planted a short kiss on my dry mouth before pressing me into the pillows with gentle force. In the next hour, she didn't leave one inch of my skin unkissed. When the tip of her tongue grazed my belly button, I pushed back my head and gave in to it. My hand caressed the small hairs at the nape of her neck until all my fingers could reach were her thick strands, and even those, I lost from my grip.

With urgent whispers of her name I begged her to quench the high that built itself gently and slowly and took possession of my body from its core, dissolving me into pieces that came together again in her arms.

A cliché.

That was the morning after.

An aching hangover in the pale light of a Sunday morning in March. Only that I was drunk from nothing but the feeling of falling asleep in her arms, her naked body wrapped around mine.

I went downstairs, downstairs where it smelled of freshly brewed coffee, and Misty. As I wrapped my arms around her to kiss her good morning, she froze.

"I can't." She cut me off before I could fathom what was happening, or why.

I withdrew my arms. She turned around, and all that was left of yesterday's look was the bewilderment. Bewilderment and—hurt. Why did she look hurt? How did she dare look hurt when she had been the one pushing me away only a minute ago?

She avoided my eyes. "I have Nate. And you have your store—what if...What if people would stop—I don't think I can do this." She raised her gaze again, but I refused to accept the silent plea in her look.

"And that occurred to you *now*?"

"I should have—"

"You kissed me! Damn it, Misty, you..." My voice cracked and I gulped away the tears.

"I'm sorry. Please, please...Jules, you know I am. You know."

I shook my head. "All I know is that you kissed me. And now you—you're treating me like a...mistake."

She straightened up, and I could see how she had changed. She was on her way to her hiding place. "I told you why."

"You're doing this because of what people might think?" I laughed incredulously. I knew I was pushing her further into her shell, but I couldn't be fair in that moment. Not after I had been that happy. More than happy. So much more.

Not after I had been safe.

Her face became blank. I knew that soon, I wouldn't be able to reach her anymore. All I had were another few seconds and then...then maybe I would have lost her forever. "We've been through so much..."

She looked at me, a trace of sadness still shadowing her eyes. "But then, I had you."

I howled. "You still have me!" *And maybe more than ever.*

Misty shook her head. "This time, it's different."

I hadn't seen or heard from her since then. And here I was, sitting on a damp bench, clouds being chased by an early spring

storm, no one around but the occasional raincoat-clad figure
walking their dog.

"I wouldn't have looked for you in any other place."

Her voice warmed some place inside me that I thought I had
lost for good. She took a seat on the bench.

"If you still—I wanted to...Forgive me?" Her fingers wandered
over the wood.

I touched them with my fingertips. "You're still scared, aren't
you?"

"I am."

I nodded and interlaced our forefingers. "Me too."

For a few moments, neither of us said a word, but simply
watched our fingers slowly fumbling around each other, searching
for the old connection.

"Do I still have you?" she whispered eventually.

I looked into her face. "Of course you do." I nudged her leg
with my foot. "Stupid."

Misty threw her legs over my lap. "You're my best friend."
She beamed, taking my face in her hands.

We kissed, two lovers, two best friends on an empty beach,
and I couldn't help but think that we were such a cliché.

BLAZING JUNE

JL Merrow

It's been a proper scorcher for this early in June, and the air's thick with pollen as they break into Mrs. MacReady's. I feel like a spare part, hovering by the front door with its telltale pint of semi-skimmed sitting in a little puddle of dried-up spilled milk. If only I'd been here earlier to see it.

"Is Mrs. Mac going to prison?" Billy asks.

"No, love!" I pick him up, though he's getting too big for that really. "The police are just going in to make sure she's all right, seeing as she wasn't answering her door."

"What if she's out at the shops? Won't she be cross they've broken her window?"

"Mrs. Mac only goes out on Saturdays, when the taxi calls, remember?" He's too heavy, so I put him down before I do myself a mischief. But I keep my arm around him. "Is she all right?" I ask the male constable when he comes out again.

He gives me a smile. "Don't worry—we've called an ambulance, but I think she's just a bit dehydrated, that's all. Still, won't hurt to get her checked out."

"Did she have another fall?" I feel guilty for asking.

He nods, but he's got my meaning. "Happened before, has it? How did she manage then?"

"She's always been able to pass me a key through the letterbox, and I go in and get her back on her feet." More and more often, these days.

"Let me guess—won't trust anyone with a spare key?" The constable shrugs, like he understands what old people are like. It's a bit of a relief. "We'll have to contact social services, get her assessed. See if they think she's up to looking after herself."

I've got a fair idea how that'll go, and I feel guilty again. But it's for the best, isn't it?

"She smells funny," Billy puts in.

"Billy! What have I told you?" I turn back to the constable, and the WPC's there too now. "His dad's a tactless old so-and-so too," I say apologetically.

The WPC is about my age, probably, though I expect most people would say she looks younger. She's got pale red hair, a sort of golden colour, cropped close so that when she turns her head you can see short feathery hair at the nape of her neck. It looks soft, like velvet. Her skin's creamy-pale, and she's got a sort of lean grace to her even under all the kit the police seem to wear these days. Makes most policewomen look dumpy, but not her.

She's got a handkerchief or something wrapped round her hand, and I realise with a jolt she's bleeding. "Are you all right?"

She shrugs and smiles. It's a nice smile. "Cut myself on the window. I'll live."

"Let me look at it for you. At least wash it out." My eyes dart over to Mrs. MacReady's front door, with its peeling paint and grimy net curtains over the broken windowpane. She gets the point.

"Thanks. That's very kind of you. Mark, you're all right staying with Mrs. MacReady, aren't you?"

The constable wrinkles his nose, but he goes in anyway.

"I'm Ellen, by the way," she tells me as we step across the landing and into mine and I realise what a god-awful mess I left it in this morning.

"Carla," I say back. "And this is Billy, my little monster."

She grins. "I'm sure you're not a monster really," she says to Billy, but he goes all shy and hides behind my legs. "Must be a bit crowded for three of you, in a flat this size."

"Oh, I'm not with his dad!" I don't know why I blush. "Never was, to be honest, but VJ's a good dad to Billy. He has him every Friday—that's why I was out all day."

"Making the most of it?"

I nod. "It's my day at the gym—yeah, I know, could do with a few more of them." I carry on quickly so she doesn't feel she has to say something polite. "Then I do the shopping. No point dragging Billy round Tesco when I don't have to. But it means I'm out all day, so that's why I didn't notice the milk. Here, you run your hand under the tap while I get the first aid kit."

"Sounds like you're a good neighbour to the old dear," she says, loud so it'll carry over the sound of running water.

I'm not, really. I mean, I look in on her, and I get stuff for her when she's not up to shopping, but I always feel I ought to do more. "I try."

"Hasn't she got any family?"

I'm back with the bandages. Billy's happy enough watching TV and I don't feel bad about it, knowing he's spent the day playing footie with his dad. "She was married, but they never had any kids. I don't think she's got anyone now." I have to concentrate now, as I dab her hand dry with a clean towel and then wipe the cut with antiseptic. She's got lovely hands—long, slender fingers with short, blunt nails. Practical. Not like my bunches of sausages with nail varnish that always seems to chip as soon as I put it on.

"Sad, to be all alone like that," she says. "Goes to show, though, doesn't it? I mean, my mum's always on at me to find a man and get married, but she did all that and still ended up alone."

"Oh, not you too? That's mums for you. S'pose I'll be the same one day, pestering Billy to give me grandkids!" We both laugh, and I put the dressing on her cut. Slowly, so I don't have to let go of her hand too soon. Daft, really.

"So which gym do you go to?" she asks, not pulling her hand away or anything.

"Just the sports centre one. They do a special rate if you're on benefits." I flush. "I mean, VJ gives me what he can, but it's not enough to live on, and by the time you've paid for child care..."

She's still smiling. "I know, believe me. And anyway, what's the point of working just to pay someone else to look after your kid? He'd rather have you, wouldn't he? And who could blame him?" I'm sure she just means because I'm his mum, though her voice is soft as she says it, and she gazes into my eyes like it could mean something more.

There's a knock on the door, even though we left it open. "Ellen? The ambulance is here," the male constable calls.

"I'd better go," she says as our hands slide apart. I'd like to think there's regret in her eyes. They're pale grey, and beautiful like the rest of her. "Thanks for patching me up."

Next Friday Mrs. MacReady still hasn't come back to her flat, and I wonder if she ever will. I hope she doesn't hate me for calling the police. I've been in that flat, with its bare floorboards and crumpled newspapers. I know all she had left was her independence.

I go to the gym as usual, and it does the trick, like it always does. I don't know if it's the exercise or MTV, but when I'm in there it's like another world: no worries, just thoughts. I think about Ellen, but it's not a sad kind of longing like it has been all week, just a gentle happiness that I ever met her.

And then I see her. She walks in like a dancer, all cool and sporty in her Nike pants and vest top, so slender they drape as much as they cling. She smiles when she sees me on the exercise bike, and comes over to say hello. I'm horribly conscious of my faded breast cancer T-shirt and the saggy jogging bottoms I got for two quid down the market.

"Hi, Carla! I thought I'd give this place a try—my gym costs a fortune, and it's not all that great. Maybe we could have a coffee, afterwards?"

I pant out a yes, and she smiles again and goes off to the elliptical. It's dead ahead of me, and as she moves I can see her hips outlined, see that lovely heart shape of her bum. Her arms are pale, like the rest of her, and a little muscled, but still soft-looking.

I do an extra ten minutes on the bike without even noticing.

I'm just wondering how much longer I can string out my usual routine without making it obvious when she comes over. She still looks as cool as a spring morning, even with her face a little pink from the exercise and beads of sweat on her chest. I try not to stare at those. I must look a right state, all red-faced and panting.

"I'm ready for my shower, now—are you nearly done?" she asks, like she doesn't know.

"Yeah, I think I'll call it a day too," I say, and we walk down to the changing rooms together.

My breathing isn't getting any slower, and it's nothing to do with how fit I'm not.

I wonder how she managed to get a locker so close to mine. Maybe it's luck. Maybe someone up there does give a fart about me after all. We park our bags on the same bench, hers all smart and with a label, mine a battered old knock-off that's falling to pieces but still just about doing the job.

"You know, I like it here," Ellen says, pulling off her top. "Think I might get a membership."

She's got lovely breasts, I see as she struggles out of her sports bra. Small and perfect, with the prettiest pink nipples you ever saw. Me, I have to stand well back when I take my bra off so I don't take her eye out with one of my big bazoombas. Stretch marks on them too, not that anyone's got close enough to notice in a good long while.

"You know, when I was at school I'd have killed for a bust-line like yours," she says.

"We should've traded bodies," I tell her. "I always hated everyone looking at my chest."

"Can't blame them, though, can you?" She pulls off her Nike pants and the thong beneath, and I can't think of anything to say. She's so beautiful. So pale and willowy, like a dryad or a naiad from the stories my mum used to tell me when I was little. The hair at her crotch is darker, like ginger snaps. I wonder if she tastes as sweet.

She smiles. "I'm just dying for a shower, aren't you?"

And she grabs her towel and a couple of bottles, and pads off to the showers in her bare feet, and I just stand there with my tits out, open-mouthed.

Then I finally get my arse in gear and follow her.

* * *

She orders a latte in the cafe afterwards, and I have a cappuccino. "Have you heard anything about Mrs. MacReady?" I ask her, because it's been preying on my mind.

Ellen nods. "'Fraid so. She won't be going back to the flat. They'll find her a home. I'll let you know where."

"Thanks. I'd like to visit her." If it's not on the bus routes, maybe VJ would give me a lift, instead of to the gym on a Friday. "She's not really got anyone else." I'd like to spoon up the chocolaty froth from my cappuccino, but I don't want Ellen to think I've got no manners. Then I catch her watching me playing with my spoon with a wicked look in her eye, and I do it anyway. Her smile makes my stomach flutter.

"I think she's like us," I say. "Mrs. MacReady. I mean, she's never said so, but she told me once she only got married because she wanted kids. And then she never had any. How bloody awful is that?"

"Things are better now," Ellen says, picking up her spoon and a packet of sugar. "We've got choices she never had."

"What's it like, being a policewoman?" I ask.

She shrugs. "Oh, I dunno. What's it like being a mum?"

"It's brilliant," I tell her. "Best thing I ever did. Don't know what I'd do without my Billy, even if he can be a bit of a so-and-so sometimes. It's just—you know how relationships, sometimes they don't last? But your kid, he's yours for keeps." I go a bit red, I think. "I don't usually go on about it like this, though."

Her eyes seem to sparkle. "You should do it more often, then." She stirs her coffee, then takes out the spoon and holds my gaze as she gives it a lick before putting it on the saucer. "I always knew it'd be either the police or the army for me. Decided in the end I wasn't sure if I could actually kill anyone, if it came down to it, so the police it was."

"I bet your family is proud of you." I don't mean it to come out a bit wistful.

She just smiles again. "Oh, you know families. Never satisfied. So, you and Billy's dad, how did that happen?"

It usually hurts, when anyone asks that. And it's not that it doesn't now, but somehow, this time it's more like I'm feeling the memory of it, rather than the pain itself. "I never meant to be a single mum. I was in a relationship, had been for a couple of years, when I started trying for a baby. But when I miscarried, she couldn't deal with it. It was like she thought it was a judgment on us, or something." Or maybe she just wanted an excuse. "But when she left, I still wanted a baby. And that's when VJ said look, there's not much chance he'd be having a kid any other way, why didn't we have one together?"

"So you did. It must have been hard." Her hand brushes mine.

"Worth it, though," I say, and then I have to take a sip of my coffee because my throat's gone dry.

Ellen tells me she's got the day off, so we spend it together. Daft stuff, like walking through the park and getting ice creams. She likes vanilla, I've always gone for chocolate. They're a good mix, together. When we get back to mine she asks if she can come in. I wish I'd tidied up but it's not like she hasn't seen the mess before. There's an old film on BBC2 so we sit down to watch it, but halfway through she slides her arm around my shoulders. I don't mean to make so much of it, but when I turn in surprise it just seems natural to kiss her.

She tastes sweet, and her lips are cool and soft as ice cream. I kiss her again, worried she's going to melt away from me. Her hand comes up to cup my boob, and it's like there's a direct line sending the tingles straight down to my crotch. I'm wet for her already. I shuffle closer on the sofa, and she throws a leg over mine so she's sitting on my lap, the film forgotten and her hand still kneading my boob. I push up her T-shirt. Her skin's like velvet, with steel underneath. I don't think I've ever wanted anyone this badly.

Ellen breaks the kiss to lean back and tear off her T-shirt. I wish I had the courage to do the same but I'm not like her. I'm not beautiful, me.

Ellen does it for me, and then she undoes my bra and kisses my boobs like they're something special. "You're lovely," she says, so sweetly, so breathily I almost believe her. I can't speak, so I unhook her bra and set those perfect breasts free. Her nipples pucker and harden, so I tongue them gently to encourage them. She gasps and arches her back. Then she climbs right off me to undo her jeans and slide them down those slender hips.

I never knew what a turn-on it could be to have a beautiful, naked woman on my lap while I'm still half-dressed. From the waist down I'm perfectly respectable, at least to the naked eye, although from the waist up I'm a wanton slut. I grab her bottom, kneading the cheeks and pulling them apart.

"How long have we got?" she asks, her voice rough.

I look at the clock and work it out. Takes a bit longer than usual. "Couple of hours yet, before VJ brings Billy back."

"Then take me to bed."

"You go first," I say. I want to look at her as she walks, all fluid motion wrapped up in smooth, creamy skin. There's a tattoo of a rose on her left cheek, where only a lover would see it. I brush it lightly with my fingertips as she walks, and she shivers.

"I want to see all of you," she says when we get there, her hands on my hips and sliding up to my boobs. I undo my jeans and push them off awkwardly. At least I've got decent undies on. I never wear my worst ones when I go to the gym.

"Take those off too," she says. "I'm busy."

She is, too, kneading my boobs and brushing her thumbs over my nipples, making them stand out proud. I step out of my damp knickers and she drops to her knees, kissing her way all down my belly. My legs shiver as she nuzzles into my crotch.

"Lie down," I tell her.

"Only if you do too." She smiles and stands up, putting her arms around my waist. We kiss again, all tongues and hands, and climb onto the bed, still kissing.

I slither down, about to go down on her.

"No," she says. "Come back, I want to see your breasts."

So I use my hand on her, and she plays with my boobs, licking and sucking and biting them as she gets close. She feels like molten gold around my fingers, and when she comes she arches her back and cries like a cat. I stroke her as she comes down from it. I still can't believe she's here with me.

"Your turn," she says, and kisses her way all down me, her face still flushed and her eyes bright as diamonds. She's got a wicked tongue on her, Ellen has. It teases as much as it pleasures, keeping me on the edge so long I think I'm going to die. When I fall, I shatter, but she's there to pick me up again and hold me.

Afterwards, we lie together on the sheets, basking in the warmth of the afternoon sun, the duvet thrown to the floor. Ellen's head is on my shoulder and one hand's just playing with my boob.

"Going to miss these when you leave?" I ask. It doesn't come out as light as I'd hoped.

"I'm going to dream of these, love," she says with a smile in her voice. "Mind you keep them safe until I come round again. When can I come round again?"

Any time, day or night, but I'm not so daft as to say it. Well, maybe I am, at that. "Come whenever you can," I say.

Ellen sighs into my breast. "Wish I could say tomorrow, but I'm on lates. Shift work's a sod."

"I'm a mum, remember?" I say, pulling her closer. "I'm used to broken nights. Come when you can."

I feel her smile against my skin, and I close my eyes on the sunlight streaming through the curtains, making the dust motes dance and sparkle for joy.

June's never blazed so bright.

LEAVING

Angela Vitale

S he's the James Dean of women, cut long and lean, muscular, her words so often an understatement, her attitude so boldly owning the world. She's stepping down from my doorstep, tipping her hat, leaving. Of course, I have told her to leave, and I don't want her to go.

I bite my lip, the mixture of contradiction strong. The sky behind her is darkening down, the last flush of cerulean blue turning to cobalt on the horizon, just enough to outline her taut stance, her boi hips loose, turning away.

I, too, turn, and then steal a glance at her exiting my arched gate. I am angry to feel the fight of her in me. I fight the urge to finalize the torment of her leaving. Instead, I pick up my phone.

Moving down the hall toward my bedroom, I hear her phone ring out my window, with my ring tone, just as she opens the Chevy door. I can see her truck's shape through my fence boards.

"Hey..." she answers, her voice low and rough.

"T, close the door. Come around the back of your truck." I wait, watch her feet lumber, move and plant. "Climb up in the flatbed, T." She's moving so slowly, it looks like she's on a tranquilizer. I wonder if it is because she is sad she is leaving.

"Look over the fence, I have something to show you," I announce.

"Oh shit." Her voice drops on *shit*. "Your neighbors are gonna bust me."

"T," I call out. "I'll make it worth your while."

I watch her shape shift through my horizontal wide wood window blinds. She grabs a branch of the elm tree to pull herself up.

I angle the shade of the bedside light to shine on me inside the house like a spotlight. I set the phone down. I trace my fingers up over my hair and down the sides of my dress. I push my breasts up and together into their closest resemblance to a double-D. I pull them apart and catch a nipple between my fingers, then roll the tip deliberately between my forefinger and thumb. I let out a low, loud gasp.

"Shit, Ang." Her voice rolls low and hushed from the receiver. I lift the hem of my dress, pulling it up in grades, enjoying it in my fists, knotting them, twirling them so that the hem rises slowly up the long thickening contour of my thighs. I turn, my back to her, and bend, lift my dress above the curve of my cheeks.

"I don't think I was done with you, T," I purr into the speakerphone. "I have to leave you with this." I lift my dress from my body. It catches over my head, blocking my eyes. I turn against the windowpane. I feel the breeze hush across my breasts, her gaze like a muscle on the wind.

I toss the dress. It's a tiny, flimsy thing. I press one of the twins to the cold, hard glass, smashed to the surface like a lens, the light searing around it, a halo. I push myself back from the glass and fall on the bed in the classic XX mud-flap pose, displaying my profile, back arched, one knee lifted, breasts bare and high. I flirt my legs and give them a playful kick. I hold position. Flirt. Kick. Then pivoting, I face her, and spread my proud legs into a wide-open V. I am exposed, every inch of me lit. I'm enjoying it. I trace my fingers from the arch of each foot up the inside of each leg. Tipping my V sideways, I fold one arm through a contortionist move, my upper arm tucked under my inner thigh, my thigh high on my shoulder and circling back around far enough for my hand to give one solid smack to my butt. Punctuation. I blow her my sexiest, final kiss. Then I fold my legs and turn over and turn out the light. In the dark, I lean back and press a pillow over my eyes and mouth as if to stifle the desire that hides in me. I push another pillow between my legs... I am going to have to make peace with solitude. I roll over and moan. I push the silence, fabric and loft until it covers and drowns my sensation.

When I get up to get a glass of water, I smell her cologne, that clean scent on the wind. Sure I am imagining it, I am shocked when I turn the corner and smack into her in the hall. She grabs me around the waist and I scream. "You're gonna get it." Her voice is a playful, low, confident threat, threaded with that cold undercurrent that confounds safety, that mixes up warmth with danger. I turn around and run. She catches me. Our lips find each other with their rough hunger.

The hall is dark, dimly lit only by streetlights. She pins my hand and pushes me to the wall, pulls my hips toward her and leans into them squarely. She's hung, and I feel the push of it. My feet climb and push against the opposite wall, straddling her. She pushes her weight into me, covers me and presses my back up.

"I'm not finished with you," she rumbles, and the top of her hand lifts into my pussy while the other begins to pull loose the five-button latch on her jeans. In my creamy wetness, like a fruit, she frees her sex and pushes herself into me in the hall. The thrusting contrast of hard and soft is driving me crazy, her thumb moving in slow, round, wet circles on my clitoris. I come quickly, collapsing in her arms, and she holds me a moment.

When I catch my breath and stop crying, she grasps my wrist roughly, tenderly, and pulls me down the hall. She pushes me toward my room and folds me face-down over the bed, my legs still right-angled to the ground. There's a ferocity to her now. From the toy chest, she is fixing something larger into her harness, the tension of her wrist changing as it holds me, her other arm moving. I push back against her.

"On the bed," she yells, and it feels like the first time she has yelled at me. I feel little, like I'm in trouble, something close to cowering, suddenly aware of the long length between me and the ceiling, the magnitude of the bed. I move, scoot up, her voice taking me into subspace. Her hand comes down smartly, sharply, across my behind. Her spanking thuds through my pelvis and thighs. I draw up. The impact reverberates through my lips and cunt. I feel the sharp sting of it like chili peppers on my skin. I lose my breath. My lips engorge, and she fixes her eyes on them. They are engorged and pulsing. She runs her hands possessively across my red skin. I am trembling, and get goose bumps.

She turns me over onto my back. Her hand travels down my thighs. She pushes my knees out, increment by increment. We are in slow motion. My labia swell. I am like cake in an oven, my pelvis, my clitoris, my G-spot, all rising, leavening, my cunt like egg batter, drippy and rich.

With my legs spread in a rough diamond, she puts one hand along my neck and one hand on my cunt, cupping it, and pushes herself into me again. She slides in, teasing me, teasing me more, and then she drives her dick home, burying herself hilt, pommel, hunger, and need.

My head rolls back and the length between my hips and shoulders lengthens. I am in love with the feeling of taking her in. I meet each push without resistance, with a flush that flowers in me, grows, and relaxes me wider. She is pushing her tongue into my mouth, whirling it. I fight the urge to gag, and open further, my mouth, my cunt the same channel. She is moving herself slowly but aggressively all the way into the gush between my legs, easing out and pushing in, coming again, gathering momentum, and pushing, falling against that place that fills me. I arch and push my G-spot down, my cunt, my hair, her breaths coming in quick succession. She hooks her arms under my shoulders and pushing, in a final cry, shudders. It's my body now, racked, and racking, the cry crescendoing through me, tears rolling through my shoulders, down my cheeks, a crashing wave that crushes the bed frame and washes all the bedroom walls. Our bodies are wet with sweat and come.

She pulls out of me and slips off the harness. I curl around and push my butt back into her. I hitch up into her hips and pull her arm around my waist. The hush of night becomes a rocking of the crickets. I pull the covers across us. I turn and cradle her head to my breast.

In two hours, I will wake and hear her truck start, and the gravel of the road will kick up gently under her wheels. No light in the sky. When I awaken again, she'll be on a plane, in the air, and I'll have to fight my anger all over again. I'll push the pillow between my thighs and another one over my eyes, and dream up yet another new set of seductions to sustain us.

FLASH FREEZE

Giselle Renarde

They keep saying food prices are on the rise, but I never thought I'd feel the pinch so soon. Times like these, I miss my old job, my old life—a dog groomer's wage doesn't cover much more than the rent. I miss the little luxuries, like blueberries and Häagen-Dazs. After buying groceries for the week, the change in my pocket isn't even enough to grab a coffee. Two quarters, one dime, and three pennies. I feel them freezing my thigh through the cotton membrane of my jeans pocket. There was a time, not long ago, when I could afford cappuccinos with whipped cream and caramel drizzle.

My whole face is a big block of ice, even after I duck inside my threadbare scarf. Icicles form against my nose hairs where my breath freezes before it can escape. *Pretty bloody sexy.* I need new mittens too—I knitted these myself, and they've got big gaps where I slipped stitches. In all these years, I've never figured out how to fix my mistakes. Fixing mistakes requires more humility than I will ever, ever possess. But life goes on.

God, what I wouldn't give to hold something hot in my hands right now. The wind is howling, ghostly, cutting through my hat and burning my ears. There are three coffee shops between here and home, and I won't be stopping at any of them. I cut down a residential street to avoid the temptation. The radio's been saying gas prices are going up, too, every day in fact, but I don't need to know that. I don't own a car.

Adjusting my reusable shopping bags on my shoulders, I watch my winter boots step across thick sheets of ice on the sidewalk. Careful, careful. Don't want to fall. Yesterday it was like spring. It rained for hours and the fashionistas wore their eighty-dollar galoshes to avoid these puddles that, overnight, turned into ice fields. Flash freeze. Everything that was gushing and warm yesterday is frozen solid today. She's unpredictable, that trickster Nature. Can't count on anything when she's in town.

I look up as I cross the street, and my heart freezes too. The one part of me that isn't affected by the weather does tend to clamp down in the face of subtler things. And Zarina has always been subtle.

Fuck! I'm standing in the middle of the goddamn road, thanking God there's no traffic on this street, and watching Zarina slide across the sidewalk like she's got skate blades underneath her retro high-tops. *In the eighties, she wasn't even born yet.* The thought weirds me out, but she acts so much older than her twenty-one years. Sometimes. And other times she behaves just like a child.

I can't let her see me.

Rushing across the street, I do my damnedest to cut over to the next block. My feet are not cooperating, and I feel like a cartoon character, sliding and jumping, limbs flailing in every direction, oranges flying out of my bag and rolling down the sidewalk. Sooner or later it was bound to happen, and apparently today's the day. My boots slide out from under me and I go down hard. My ass smacks the ice and my head the cold cement. All I can do is lie there staring up at the bare branches, black against a grey-blue sky. Maybe it'll snow later.

"Oh my God!" I hear her voice, but I don't think she knows it's me just yet. "Oh my God, are you okay?"

I feel her footfalls as she runs up from behind me, tumbling to her knees at my side. She looks like a Persian princess, with the widest dairy-cow eyes I've ever seen, which only grow wider with recognition.

"Lauren," she says, gasping. "Oh my God, are you okay?"

Her long black hair cascades over one shoulder. It's one of the coldest days of the year and she isn't wearing a hat. That almost makes me angry because I care for her so damn much. And *that* definitely makes me angry, because after what she did to me I don't want to care for her at all.

I moan, trying to ease myself up off the concrete, but my head feels just too heavy. I try to convey *yes, I'm fine*, but all that comes out is, "Ahhhh."

"Can you move?" she asks. There's panic in her eyes. "I can call an ambulance."

"No," I grunt, forcing myself up. Once I'm sitting, I feel too dizzy to function. I let my head fall into her lap, which is the only place it ever really wanted to be, anyway.

"Lauren!" she shouts. "Oh my God, I'm calling nine-one-one."

Summoning every ounce of strength my barely conscious mind can generate, I sit up again and say, "No, I'm okay." The cold wind slaps me in the face and I feel...not *better*, but at least a little less sleepy. I want to throw up, but I don't let myself. Not in front of her.

Slipping my arms out of my grocery bags, I force my legs

to carry my weight, and they do, but like those of a newborn giraffe. Zarina stands too, and I let my body sink into hers, chest to chest, our skin separated only by her pea coat, my bomber jacket, and a whole lot of sweaters. Still, it's the closest we've ever been. I hook my chin around her shoulder and suddenly there are tears streaming down my face, freezing against my cheeks. Their warmth fresh from my eyes hurts more than their frigidity once they ice over, and I don't know why I'm crying but I can't seem to stop.

She says, "I think you have a concussion," and I think, *How would you know? What are you, a doctor?* and then I feel guilty for being mean to her, even just in my head.

"I think so too," I reply, wishing my arms would wrap around her body like hers are wrapped around mine. My muscles won't follow instructions. I've never felt so helpless in all my life.

Zarina picks up my grocery bags and flings them both over the same shoulder. Of course I think to offer my help, but I know I just can't manage it. I'm not even sure I can walk.

"You still live on Isabella?" she asks.

She remembers where I live. "Yeah, the building on the corner."

But of course she remembers. We walked home together enough times after work. *Work*...ah, the halcyon office job days. Our little firm handled immigration, primarily, but also some family law and real estate to bring in the cash. Zarina started there with a co-op placement when she was still in high school and they hired her on as administrative assistant right after she graduated. Those were good years. I loved working there, until it all fell apart. And it all fell apart because of Zarina.

I'm not exactly sure how we get from the street where her father lives back to my building, but she's asking for my keys, so it must have happened somehow. I don't feel cold anymore.

Now I'm warm…too warm…and I'm afraid of what will happen when she leaves. She's still lugging my groceries on one shoulder and lugging me on the other, my forehead resting against her woolly white scarf. She smells like springtime, and I wonder if that's just my hope for a thaw as I follow her into the elevator.

"What floor are you on?" she asks. She's never actually been inside my apartment.

"Sweet sixteen," I mumble. It's funnier in my head. I don't tell her that I had to move to a different suite after I left my office job. I couldn't afford a one-bedroom anymore, not in this part of town, and not washing dogs for a living. The new one is a bachelor, but the southern view is spectacular. You can see all the way to the lake.

She drags me from the lift. I don't know how I'm still standing. "Which one's yours?"

I lead her to the threshold, hoping she'll come through with me. She opens my door and I laugh my ass off when all I smell is wet dog. Laundry's been building up over the past week and I just couldn't be bothered.

"Nobody's seen this apartment but you," I tell her as I fall to my knees in the entryway. It feels so good to be home that I put my head down on the cream-coloured carpet and close my eyes. I'm floating now, with a light, fluffy cloud carpet under my face, and I sigh in relief.

I hear Zarina whisper "Fuck" as she falls to her knees beside me for the second time today. I can't figure out why she's so upset when I'm soaring so high. She unzips my coat and unwraps my scarf. My boots come off, and my hat, my homemade mittens… she takes off everything but my leggings and my undershirt. I smell worse than a wet dog, but I get the sense she doesn't care. She's muttering, and I hear what she's saying but nothing registers except her concern.

She drags me by my armpits across the carpet, and when we get to my bed I say, "I can do it," and crawl under the covers. Nothing in the world has ever felt this good. I close my eyes and smile, and I'm so damn happy I don't even care that every time I start to drift off Zarina shouts, "Lauren," and flicks me on the forehead. It feels like a game, and I laugh.

My head is heavy like a brick and it drags me down into the past, back to the old days. I wasn't in the closet, but I wasn't out at work. I'd always compartmentalized my life anyway, so I didn't feel like who I favoured romantically had any bearing on my job. There was a real estate agent, Phil, who brought us a lot of clients—a big part of my job as a paralegal was coordinating closings—and Phil was the kind of gay guy you could spot a mile away. His outness really put me at ease, because I'd never been good with guys. I know it sounds like a lesbian stereotype, but most men just rub me the wrong way. Even my boss Fazil bugged me when I first started working for him. Then, over time, I observed how he interacted with Phil. Nobody else seemed to notice, but I did, and I got more comfortable around him. We became friends, even. He was married, and he assured me he wasn't interested in me "that way," so I told him I was queer and I didn't like him "that way" either. We became close friends. Intimate friends. And he admitted to me he was having an affair with Phil. He'd enjoyed trysts with men before, but now he was falling in love. Nobody else knew. It was our little secret.

I'm not one to judge because, shit, I've been there and then some. When I was young and naïve, I fell in love with a married woman, so I knew where Fazil was coming from. For a while, I even thought she'd leave her husband for me. When I realized that was never going to happen, I was shattered. I put my heart in the deep freeze because that seemed the safest place for it. Maybe that's why I focused so much of my energy on my job and why I didn't feel like being out at work was relevant. It's not like I was dating anyone. I'd shut my heart down. Until Zarina.

It wasn't just that she was beautiful, or funny, or clever, or quirky. She was one of those genuinely kind people you don't often encounter, certainly not in a law office. Though I was ten years older than her, I felt young when she was around. We all did, I think. She brought us music and style. She woke us up. Everybody liked her. In fact, everybody seemed to like her the same way I did, and a year after coming on full-time, she started dating our very own partner-by-age-thirty-five, a guy named Dennis. He was okay, or so I thought, but I really thought there was something between Zarina and me, and my heart felt trampled once again when she chose him over me. Not that I ever made a move or offered any suggestion I was interested. In truth, of course, I was scared of being let down again. Nobody likes to get hurt.

In the midst of my intense Zarina crush and the ensuing disappointment, I clung harder to Fazil for support. He had grown deeper in love with Phil, and there was no one else he could talk to about that relationship. On the days Zarina couldn't walk me home because she was going out with Dennis, Fazil and I hung around at work, drinking in his office. Without him, I'd have drowned my sorrows alone, and I would have felt like the world's biggest loser doing that. I loved him for the support he showed me. He was such a good friend.

And then the rumour started. Fazil and I had chosen to hide our friendship, to a degree, because we knew how it would look, and he wasn't ready to stand up at work and say, "I'm in love with another man." As it turned out, that would have helped my case immensely.

It's strange to hear things about yourself and know they're

not true, but also know there's no way real to dispute them. *Fazil and Lauren are having an affair*. That's what everybody thought. I'd catch hints of whispers, titters, snarky comments coming from God-knows-where, and it made me so damn angry because who could I confront? How do you deal with something that's floating in the air? Fazil was my boss, and suddenly I felt awkward just walking into his office because I knew all eyes were on us.

"What are we going to do about this?" I asked him one day.

Fazil looked at me pleadingly, but he didn't say anything.

I was reaching the end of my tether. "We have to do something. I get the feeling my job's hanging by a thread, here. The partners keep finding fault in everything I do. It's like they're setting me up."

Fazil shook his head and then nodded for me to look out his door. Dennis strode across the expanse of the office, eyes dark, heading this way. Zarina stood behind her little desk, watching, on high alert. The second we made eye contact, she looked down into a file folder, guilty as sin, and that's when I knew she had started the rumour. It was Zarina. The knife stuck in my back as I looked down at Fazil, who seemed so small in that moment. Scared.

In about five seconds, something was going to crash, but I'd be damned if he came down with me.

Pushing past Dennis, I stepped up on my wobbly office chair and stood on my desk in the office's main space. Picking up my coffee cup and the spoon from my yogurt, I banged the one against the other like I was calling for a toast. This was it. I was throwing myself under the bus. "Attention, attention, I'd like to make an announcement. I just want everybody to know that, contrary to popular belief, I am in fact a big dyke. One hundred percent grade-A lesbian, always have been, always will be, so all you assfaces who accused me of having an affair with my boss need to get your heads out of the toilet and start concentrating on your work. Whatever you're paid, it's too much if you spend your days gossiping about coworkers."

I was still going on about how "you could ruin people's lives, and you don't even give a fuck, do you?" when Dennis grabbed me by the arm and pulled me down from my desk. I landed with a less than graceful thud and let him drag me into his office, because I wasn't done yet. If Zarina had started this rumour, surely he had his part. They were a couple, after all.

"Enough of this," he said when the door was closed. I wouldn't sit down. I felt like a high school kid in the principal's office. If only I'd had a wad of gum to stick under his desk. "Look, you're right about office gossip, but pretending to be something you're not is pretty low. Just end it with Fazil and we'll pretend this never happened."

There were a lot of things I expected Dennis might say, but that was definitely not on the list. I was speechless, at first. I really didn't know how to respond. "You think...I'm lying?"

He was so slick and easy as he tossed himself into the leather chair on the other side of his desk. "Come on, Lauren, I know you're not gay."

That word sounded bizarre. "I didn't say I was gay, I said I was a lesbian."

With a smug smile painted across his lips, he shook his head. "Look, I have no problem with gay people. Phil, you know, the real estate guy? He's gay and I think he's great, but you can't pretend to be gay to wriggle your way out of an accusation."

I made a sound like, "Whaaaa?" but Dennis couldn't seem to cut the shit.

"I know lots of lesbians," he claimed, looking me up and down. "They don't look like you."

The knot in my belly erupted, and I was halfway to my desk before I realized I was laughing. I could feel the tears welling up in my eyes, but I wouldn't let them spill just yet. Pulling my purse from my bottom drawer, I yanked out a subdued shade of pink lipstick and scribbled *I QUIT* on the wall above my desk. When my lipstick broke, I grabbed a Sharpie and followed that up with *go fuck yourselves hard*. It wasn't clever, but I was angry and thinking on my feet.

I wished Fazil good luck as I stormed past his office—he was still seated slack-jawed behind his desk—and when I turned to push the door open with my back, my gaze locked with Zarina's. She stood like an arrow outside Dennis's office, her plump lips parted, her brow streaked with lines of disconcertion. I'd never seen her eyes so wide, until today.

Zarina's flicking my forehead now and I bat her hand away like a kitten. She smiles, but her eyes are still heavy with worry. "I put your groceries away," she says, "and the kettle just popped. Want some tea?"

"Do I want some hot chocolate?" I ask. I'm less mature now than I was when we met, plus my body wants sugar.

She sighs as she slides off my bed, walking to the little kitchen nook. "I really think I should call a doctor. There's something wrong with you."

"It took you this long to figure that out?"

Turning from my cupboards, she gives me a smirk, and my whole body feels alive. While she searches unaided for mugs and hot chocolate mix, I gently remind myself why I don't like her: she spread that rumour about me and Fazil, she never called me or stopped by after I quit even though she lives three streets down the block, and worst of all she's dating the assface who didn't believe I was a lesbian. He'd be pleased with my appearance now, I'm sure. I cut my hair, pierced my eyebrow, I never wear skirts anymore, and I've got him to thank. *Cheers for the complex, Dennis!*

"How's your *boyfriend*?" The words hurl themselves across my apartment like airborne venom. I hate myself for asking, but I blame the concussion.

Zarina turns from the kettle, and her expression tells me she has no idea what I'm talking about. "Dennis," I clarify, though I still feel like a jerk.

She laughs, and then groans. "Oh God, don't remind me!" She picks up two mugs and wanders slowly toward the bed, spilling a little hot chocolate on my carpet. "Oops. Sorry. I'll clean it up."

"Don't worry," I blurt, wanting to know, hoping, praying, wishing she might be available. "It's okay, just...what happened?"

I sit up in bed and she hands me a mug, snuggling in next to my hip. I feel her warmth and her sweetness through the covers, and Zarina does more for me than the cocoa. "I quit right after you left," she tells me. "Everybody heard what Dennis said to you. He was a jerk. You know, he was the one who started that whole rumour about you and Fazil. His first wife had cheated on him, and he was just really sensitive to that stuff. Not that I'm making excuses. It was so brave of you to come out like that, and he cut you right down."

Sheepishly, I admit, "Well, I got a nice severance cheque in the mail. I guess they didn't want the Ministry of Labour involved, or whatever." But I feel awful, now, that I held a grudge all this time and it wasn't Zarina at all. "I'm sorry you lost your job because of me."

She pets my arm as I sip my hot chocolate. She's already put her mug down on my night table, and she moves in closer, consoling me. "It wasn't your fault. Fazil gave me a good reference, and I found a better job pretty quickly. I just got so mad.

If he didn't believe you, I knew he wouldn't believe me, and he didn't."

"What do you mean?" I ask as she takes the mug from my hands and sets it down. I think I know, but I want to be sure. I've never been one to take chances.

With a half shrug, Zarina sets her head down on my chest. All I feel is her warmth, and all I smell is the springtime in her hair. "I've always been more attracted to girls than guys. I dated Dennis, and I dated other boys before him, but I thought..." She chuckles, but there's a wry quality to it. "I just thought that's what women did: fell in love with other women, but dated men because... because we're supposed to. I think I always believed that until..." She gazes up at me like a fawn, and my heart soars with her breath, though I can't seem to breathe myself. "Until you quit, that day. It was one of those *don't know what you've got till it's gone* things."

My head is pounding, but I can't conceive of a more perfect moment. I take that chance I never take, and I ask, "You fell in love with a woman?"

Her bottom lip trembles, and tears soak her eyes as she falls across my chest. "I should have come after you when you left. I should have told you how I felt, but I was scared. I should have stopped Dennis from saying all those things about you. I knew in my heart you were different, and you weren't having an affair with Fazil, and if you were going to have an affair with anyone it would be with..."

She sobs against my breast, and I want nothing more than to applaud the risk she's taken. Now I'm doing the consoling, running my fingers through her long hair and whispering, "Shh, honey, it's okay. It's okay now."

All at once, she stops and lifts her head, gazing into my eyes. "I should have done it a different way."

"It's not too late," I tell her, feeling at once young and maternal. "You take care of me tonight, keep flicking my forehead and bringing me sweet drinks, and I'll take care of you every night after. How about that?"

She smiles and then laughs, her cheeks streaked red but her eyes gleaming like diamonds. I can't say I never expected to see her again, seeing as she lives three streets away, but I don't think I anticipated falling on the ice trying to get away from her, only to be taken into her care. It occurs to me that I might be dead, or in a coma, or dreaming, and a sudden panic makes my heart race. Then she leans in close and sets her lips against mine, and I know this moment is real.

DUMB BUNNY

Lee Lynch

F renchy had been retired less than a year when the store asked her to come back to train a new employee.

"They begged," she'd bragged to Clove over coffee at Café Femmes. Clove had a live-in girlfriend, so they were just friends right now. Outside the plate glass window, umbrellas covered everyone except for a swarm of little kids headed home from school.

"Does that stop your pension?"

Frenchy sipped her latte, savoring the telling of her new title. She'd only told her brother over the phone. He'd whistled and asked if she would still come to Florida that winter. "I called the shots when they offered me the job and made it a condition of employment," she'd answered. "Told them I'm practically a snowbird now." Serge had laughed. She really only went down there to house-sit for him and his wife so they could travel, but she'd been thinking of getting a little condo of her own down there. This part-time work would help.

"I still get my pension checks and health coverage," she said to Clove. Then she whispered, "I'm the Training Consultant. Thirty-five an hour. I told them I wouldn't take less."

Clove was watching a driver back his rig up to a loading dock across the street. "Should have held out for forty. That's a big job."

Clove reminded her of Mercedes that way—she always found the negative. Her mother had been like that too. "I get travel time," she said, hating herself for being so defensive. "That's the only part I don't like—the trainee works all the way over in Staten Island. The company pays for a car service, though. Door to door."

"Why don't you get that boastful look off your face, short stuff. You know the company's saving money on you somehow."

She glowered at Clove, but Clove insisted. "When I was your cashier? Look at all the hours they got out of you free, just for letting them call you Store Manager."

Of course Clove had been right, Frenchy admitted as she boarded the ferry. On the other hand, the company would have had a driver take her all the way to Staten Island today, but she liked to go by boat. There would be a car waiting for her on the island side.

"This is a tough one," her boss had told her on the phone, "but that's why we wanted you back, Genevieve."

"It's what I get for being good at my job. You guys are always throwing me the hard balls."

Her boss had cleared his throat and continued, "You're going to train Dom Sausilito's daughter, Muriel."

"He's trusting me with his daughter?" she'd cried in alarm. Dom owned the whole chain. "Does he know I'm...you know."

"Yeah, he knows you're gay and he knows you don't want to lose your pension."

How, she puzzled, could they take her pension away? It wasn't worth risking that just to feel useful again. She had her SAGE members, two of them, to visit every week. She figured she'd need Services and Advocacy for Gay Elders someday too. She was in charge of food for the women's dances and she was on her co-op board again this year. Once every couple of months she got together with Mercedes, always a little bit hopeful she could rekindle the old spark they'd shared, but afraid of it too. On the other hand, she couldn't turn down her boss. She loved him like a father—sometimes.

"Not a prob," she said aloud. "Dom's, what, seventy-something? How old is this daughter?"

"That's the strange part, Genevieve. She's fifty-three and she's kept house for him since she was in her teens. Dom calls her Bunny, by the way, and that's what she goes by."

"Bunny? What kind of name is Bunny?"

Of course Dom, who was from Staten Island, would want his daughter close, she thought when the car dropped her off. She plucked a dark thread off the sleeve of her brand-new white shirt, shrugged into her red blazer with the gold crest, and told the driver to come get her four hours later. No cashier took more than four hours to train.

This Staten Island Apple Cart was brand new, with wide, clean aisles. The trainee was adorable: small, but curvy. Really curvy under that slightly gaping lemon yellow blouse she wore. Bunny remarked on their nearly identical navy blue slacks. She was all pink and white like her name, Bunny. Her skin was completely unwrinkled and she wore gold wire-rimmed glasses. Bunny would have looked about thirty-five except for the fine short early white hair, like a rabbit's fur, only curly. Frenchy wanted to pet it. Not enough to lose her pension, though.

She first suspected Bunny wasn't a very worldly person when

Bunny went hunting for number keys on the cash register.

"Oh, Frenchy, I feel so silly," Bunny declared in her breathy, little-girl voice, small in the noise of canned music and the coolers, refrigerators, blowers, chatting customers, and electric shopping scooters. "I should have known there wasn't a number eleven key from using calculators!"

Was Bunny kidding? She nodded in case she wasn't, to show her it wasn't such a bad mistake, though the truth was that it was the first time she'd run into it. Bunny would definitely not have been hired if she was doing the hiring.

Yet when Bunny babbled, as she seemed to like to do, Frenchy found herself smiling. It was like listening to an excited child on her first day of school. The woman was always cheerful. She never said anything against her father for the years she'd lost while taking care of him even though, now that he had remarried, he was making her go to work.

"He says it's good for me," Bunny explained. "He says who knows how long he'll be around and I should work till I'm seventy to get good social security, so I guess he's leaving his money to Krista. She'll have longer than me to use it." From which Frenchy eventually deduced that the new wife was younger than the daughter. Maybe Clove was right about the owner being a bum. Or maybe Bunny was joking.

"Ooh, Frenchy, look at that. You don't want to pay me $5,002.35, do you?" Bunny asked the customer with a smile that made her look helpless. It took Frenchy a good two minutes to fix the cash register error.

Over the next weeks, as four hours turned into four hours a day, she learned that she hadn't seen everything on this job after all. Working at the store hadn't rattled her in years, but Bunny had a knack.

"Ooh, Frenchy, Frenchy," Bunny called when Frenchy was

talking to the third key manager, a guy who wanted Bunny out of his store yesterday, owner's daughter or not. The third key was telling her how Bunny had mangled the price changes the week before.

"What is her problem, Frenchy? Anybody could figure out that eighteen cents is the price increase, not the price."

Bunny had a yard of register tape wrapped around her wrist.

"Oh, Frenchy, I'm all thumbs when it comes to changing the tape."

The customers were looking at one another, jiggling keys and craning their necks for a shorter line.

For the life of her, Frenchy could not find what Bunny had done or how to fix it. She apologized to the customers and had Bunny herd them to the next register where she signed herself on and played cashier at top speed. Bunny bagged and entertained the customers with funny stories about her mistakes.

"This woman," Frenchy complained later to her long-distance girlfriend Gloria, who had called as she got on the ferry the first evening of daylight savings time. The city was dressing itself up in lights for Friday night outside her window. "She's not dumb."

"She sounds dumb," countered Gloria.

"She's nervous. She's good with numbers, just not with machines. She tells me she can cook like a chef."

"Has she asked you over to demonstrate?" The amusement in Gloria's voice came through all the way from Texas. "And don't tell me you wouldn't go, even if she wasn't the owner's daughter."

"Of course I wouldn't go. I'm not dumb either."

That weekend when she went home with Bunny for a celebration dinner, she remembered what she'd told Gloria. Bunny had made it through an entire shift with under three mistakes, though, which was the goal Frenchy had set for her.

Was Bunny always this easily excited? You would have thought she'd won a gold in the Olympics the way she chattered. Frenchy had never known anyone with such a sunny attitude, or who was so open about her failings. She was right, too, about being a great cook.

"Daddy always said that he'd have to hire a chef to replace me if I ever found a guy who wanted to steal me away. As if."

A guy? She was surprised by how disappointed she felt. "As if what?"

"I'd leave him!"

"But he just left you."

Bunny frowned. "I never thought of it like that."

She was pretty, Dom's daughter. It was a gentle prettiness, nothing to knock you flat and everything to do with that sweet, if sometimes clueless, smile. She wanted to kick Dom the next time she saw him, for holding this woman hostage to his loss when her mother died. If that wasn't some form of abuse, she didn't know what was.

He must have bought her this great apartment out of guilt, because Bunny sure wasn't paying for it on cashier pay. She had two bedrooms, both doors closed. Bunny had explained that her society finches had the run of one room. They were chattering nonstop, like Bunny. Plug-in air fresheners pumped out the scent of oranges. Once again, Frenchy watched lights come on in the city, this time from the twelfth floor of a high-rise not far from the water.

"I have a park nearby," Bunny was saying as she cut an avocado in half, extracted the stone, and deftly peeled it. Based on Bunny's problems at the store, Frenchy cringed every time the knife neared her thumb, in particular when she skinned the cuke, leaving strips of green to alternate with the pale flesh, but she was an expert in the kitchen.

"Do you like rice vinegar?" Bunny asked.

"Never had it."

"Ooh, it's so good. It's my favorite. And here, just some dill and the salad's all ready for the fish."

She was sitting on a stool across the counter from Bunny, who turned to heat up a ribbed cast iron pan, something else new to Frenchy. She felt so relaxed she could lay her head down and nap right there. To keep herself awake she asked about the pan.

"It was Mommy's."

Could this woman really be a New Yorker, with her openness and childlike confidence? Bunny brushed olive oil on salmon fillets, then salted and peppered them from grinders, not shakers. She was so quick, yet so careful, like a musician doing a tune she'd played a hundred times before.

"See," Bunny said with an authority that transformed her small voice, "you make the oven real hot, to about five hundred degrees. Then you heat the pan and," she dipped into a salt cellar with a tiny spoon, "you sprinkle salt on it."

"I feel like I'm watching a cooking show on TV."

"What a nice thing to say. But look, it's smoking. This is when you put the fish in the pan and slide it onto the bottom rack of the oven."

Frenchy watched Bunny's bottom, in clingy black pants, as she bent.

"Now, you be the timekeeper while I set the table." Bunny also slid a CD into her miniature sound system. Smooth jazz, maybe Grover Washington. Bunny turned suddenly back to Frenchy. "Ooh! What a terrible hostess I am! You're my first guest ever in my own place, and I didn't ask if you want soda or juice."

Bunny bustled back and forth to the dining area. Frenchy

couldn't get over how calm she felt inside, how easily she breathed, how a smile spread so naturally on her mouth. Bunny had a motherliness to her, except for that heavenly body.

"Frenchy," Bunny scolded as she hurried back to the stove. "You're not keeping time very well."

She chuckled at the scolding.

"Perfect!" Bunny flipped the fish without splashing her bright yellow pullover top with the lacy scoop neck the way Frenchy would. "I guess I'll forgive you. This time."

Would there be other times? She found herself hoping so. Then she recognized Bunny's tone. Was the owner's daughter being just a little bit flirtatious?

Two minutes later Bunny had the fish out of the oven and was chunking it into the salad. Bunny let her carry it to the table.

"Candles? Would you like candles?" Without waiting for an answer, Bunny lit two almond-scented candles that were already on the table and dimmed the overhead light. Did a woman who was into guys do that for a girl guest?

Frenchy hardly said a word through dinner, except to praise the pleasure of a home-cooked meal, while Bunny talked about the store, her sad performance, Frenchy's patience with her. When she asked how Bunny's dad was, Bunny launched into a blow-by-blow of his health and little stories about him that made them both laugh.

"We could never just go somewhere," Bunny told her. "If we were visiting family out on Long Island, Daddy had to stop at the grocery stores. Not every one, but one or two each time. He'd drive an hour out of the way to check on a new chain or a remodeled supermarket. He'd rant about his pet peeves—like food stores built into malls. 'Ridiculous,' he'd yell. 'Your grocery is going to be your last stop, right?' Like he was really asking me. 'If the customer goes to Macy's and Sears and the food court first, what do they have left? Only enough cash for the things on their list. No impulse items, no stocking up while they're there. The customer is tired, isn't she? By this time the kids are cranky. The husband's worrying about all the spending. Never,' he'd tell me, 'never buy a store in a mall. Freestanding is what you want.' You don't see grocery stores in malls anymore, do you?"

"Come to think of it," Frenchy said, "you don't."

Going over to Bunny's for dinner became a habit, even after Bunny's cashier training was finished and she'd moved to Deli Clerk, then Meat Wrapper.

"You're learning to do it all," Frenchy commented when she got to the New Dorp store and Bunny was working the customer service desk.

"Ooh, Frenchy," Bunny said, her eyes happy and excited. "I'm learning so much!"

The clerk who was teaching Bunny rolled her eyes. Frenchy frowned at the clerk.

"Spreadsheets were hard for me," she told Bunny. "I couldn't get the concept."

Bunny said, "It's so much easier than keeping a log book and adding it all ourselves."

Again, the clerk rolled her eyes. But Frenchy kind of wished they could go back to the days before computers and told that to Bunny, who stopped her scurry toward the bathroom next to the customer service counter saying, "I remember when Daddy first put bathrooms in the front of his stores so the customers weren't wandering around the storage areas, maybe helping themselves. He said he'd rather put Porta-Potties in the parking lots, but the city wouldn't stand for it."

She was actually getting to like Staten Island. The people were so different from real New Yorkers, she told Bunny. That visit Bunny served a blue fish chowder she'd had in a crock pot all day and Frenchy was ready to buy the half-million-dollar apartment next door instead of anything in Florida. Could you fall for a woman because of her cooking? It was like Bunny wore food smells as perfume, and they got Frenchy feeling like a baby butch in spring.

Her Bank Street home seemed dark and lonely compared to Bunny's place, all filled with bright yet soft colors. Her place was still pretty much furnished with her original stuff. She'd been so proud of the black-and-white houndstooth check living room set she'd found at a going-out-of-business sale on Fourteenth Street—and then she'd found drapes in the exact same pattern! It all seemed so old-fashioned and dingy now, even with the gold lampshades and the diamond-patterned gold and black carpet. It smelled like unaired apartment.

There was a still life over her couch that bored her to tears. It had attracted her twenty-five years ago, but she'd been mistaken to think she'd always like it. Bunny was like a work of art you wanted to have around for a long time.

If she wasn't gay, she would ask Bunny down to Florida with her. She'd be fun to take to Disney World. They'd have to sleep in the same room together at her brother's, so that wasn't such a hot idea. Serge would think Bunny was dense just like everyone at the store thought. She was still hearing stories about Bunny's nervous goof-ups, like how she cashed a city check for someone who showed her a driver's license. When they compared the number Bunny had handwritten on the back of the check with the driver's license number pre-printed on the check, it wasn't the same. Five hundred and some odd dollars down the drain, plus bank fees.

Bunny sure knew how to bring a house alive, though, and how to light up someone's day. Those weren't qualities Frenchy had thought to value before.

She talked Florida up, surprised that Bunny had never been

there. Bunny, it turned out, had been off Staten Island less than a dozen times in her life.

"They have a name for what I have and I started on pills for it just last year."

Frenchy wasn't sure it would be more polite to ask or not to ask for details. They were at the park by the water. It was twilight and fall. She wouldn't mind putting the orange and red leaves, the peach sunset streaked with narrow yellow clouds and jet plumes and the blue water with pink highlights, on her wall.

"You think there's a poster of this?"

"Of the sunset?"

"From Staten Island." She felt it, that they weren't holding hands, as they stood side by side. She wasn't used to hanging out with straight girls.

"You're nice to change the subject, Frenchy."

"From what?"

"From what I'm sick with."

She stopped at a bench and sat, patting the space next to her until Bunny joined her. "Tell me."

It was the first time Bunny had ever looked upset. Was it the effect of light seeping out of the sky and the damp bay air, or had a look of fear replaced Bunny's customary calm?

"Geeze. Geeze. Geeze. You're crying," she said to Bunny. "I didn't mean to make you cry."

"You didn't, Frenchy. I never told anyone outside the family before. I have a mental health problem, an anxiety disorder."

"Are you sure? You get nervous at the store, but you keep going no matter what."

"When it comes on I'm scared to leave my bed, much less my apartment. It makes me sick. I have to get to the bathroom, but I'm paralyzed with fear. I used a lot of tranquilizers at the store."

"But look at you. You're here in the park and you work at the store. You're not afraid to leave home."

"It's why I never moved out. Even when Mommy died, I was okay as long as I stayed home and kept the books."

"Not the Apple Cart books."

"You didn't know? I might be too nervous to be much good in the store, but I have a correspondence degree in accounting and enough experience working with Daddy's accountant to get my CPA license. We have services do a lot of the work, but I took over when Daddy's accountant retired. I use e-mail and fax and never leave home."

"You are one big surprise. Why didn't you tell me? Here I thought you were..."

"What? A dumb bunny?"

"Of course not," she exclaimed, ready to tell Bunny how she'd defended her to Gloria.

"Everybody thinks I'm a half-wit, Frenchy. It's okay. My counselor said I act dumb to take attention away from my social phobia. Maybe that's part of it, but also I freeze up. My brain won't work when I'm scared."

That explained it. Bunny got dumb with fear. Frenchy was supposed to make her feel safe.

"When Daddy remarried, he told me I was welcome to live with them and Krista backed him up, but you know, I didn't think that would be right. Daddy sold our big old barn of a house and moved to the top floor of the building where he bought me the apartment."

"Are you okay now, living alone?"

"Kind of. Daddy's nearby. My birds are a comfort. But as soon as I was used to being in my own place? Daddy insisted I start going out. That's why he got me the job. I'm telling you because I've felt funny all day."

"You feel funny today? So you're not over it? You're scared now?"

"Over it? I don't think that'll happen. The pills, though, help me. Some days are harder than others."

Bunny's face was pale. She seemed smaller. The poor woman looked about to hurl.

Would Bunny's father think she'd scared Bunny? "What happens to you?"

"I get so cold," Bunny said in a hoarse whisper. Frenchy could see that she was all folded in on herself, like she was under attack from a threat no one else could see. Bunny was twisting one wrist with her other hand, twisting hard so it was red. She wouldn't meet Frenchy's eyes. Her breathing was choppy.

Bunny was a mess. What the heck was she supposed to do?

"Is it happening now?" she asked.

Bunny nodded. She'd withdrawn to the farthest end of the bench, a small ghostly figure with her white hair and lavender jacket glowing in the deepening dusk.

"Should I take you home?"

"You go." Her voiced sounded like a faint growl.

"You want me to go home?"

Bunny nodded, rocking herself now. "I don't want you to see me like this."

She didn't want to see Bunny like this either. Going home sounded like a great idea, but she couldn't. "I'm not leaving you here." It was a wonder the smell of low tide wasn't making Bunny sicker. "Come on, now. The sooner you let me take you home, the sooner I'll get out of your hair."

Bunny, who had always seemed soft, warm and pliant, was hunched and stiff against Frenchy, who walked with an arm around her. This was as unsettling as being with Mercedes when she was freaking out and throwing stuff at Frenchy forty years earlier. She'd said she'd never live with another woman after that, and she hadn't.

In the elevator, Bunny shook like the last leaf in an autumn wind.

When the elevator door opened, she had to urge Bunny out and down the hall to her apartment. Then Bunny stalled on the welcome mat. Frenchy fished out keys from Bunny's purse and noticed four locks on the door. Where she lived, she could see it, but Staten Island?

Once inside, Bunny fled to the bathroom. Frenchy could hear her flushing the toilet a lot. She clicked on the TV to spare Bunny embarrassment.

When she awoke two hours later, still on the couch, the TV was off and there was a blanket over her. She wondered how much effort and courage it had cost Bunny to make those little caring gestures. The back of her forearm and her cheek were full of dents from the knobby fabric. The house smelled like a pizza parlor. Bunny, humming, looked completely normal.

"Hey," she called. She folded the blanket. "I'll get lost now. I wanted to wait and be sure you were okay, but I guess, you know, I fell asleep."

Bunny came into the living room and reached for her hands. They stood face-to-face, their arms linked between them in two v's.

"I'm so sorry," Bunny said. "When a panic attack hits I get too scared to find a pill and take it."

"Good to know," said Frenchy. "I felt kind of helpless."

"You did exactly the right thing."

"Did I say something wrong, to set it off?"

"No. I did by deciding to tell you about being sick like this." Bunny paused. "And because of the other thing I needed to tell you." She could hear Bunny's deep intake of breath. "Daddy thinks I get these because I'm gay and I'm scared to be gay out in the world."

Frenchy was stunned to silence. Bunny went on. "I was afraid you'd run off when I told you."

Running sounded good. Real good. "You told me to leave. I don't want to make it worse."

"No," Bunny said again, pulling her into a tight hug. "I don't ever want you to leave."

She'd heard that line before, but never as plaintively spoken.

It was two weeks before she next went over to Bunny's. She was nervous that Bunny would fall apart again, but Bunny was fine. Halfway there she realized she hadn't dressed up this time, although her jeans, as always, were pressed and her Yankees sweatshirt looked as new as the day she bought it.

Bunny grabbed her hand to pull her inside the apartment.

"Ooh, Frenchy, look what I found online." Bunny was in a silky electric blue shell with yellow pants this time.

On the wall across from the couch was a large framed painting that looked just like the sunset they'd watched.

"I was going to give it to you, but I hoped if I hung it here, you'd always have a reason to come back."

Frenchy swallowed. Hard. She'd decided she didn't want to be with anyone, but the sight of Bunny made her feel all warm around her heart. Bunny had been thinking about her. "You didn't need a pretty picture to get me to come back, Bunny."

"There's another reason too." Bunny's face had turned a deep pink and she looked at the cream-colored rug. "I wanted to celebrate with you again."

"Celebrate that you didn't shrink-wrap your hand in the meat-wrapping machine?" she asked with a smile.

"Oh, Frenchy. You're a tease. It's Daddy's announcement. The reason he's had me working in the store all these months."

"What?" Frenchy asked, thinking it was Bunny who was the tease.

"Daddy's convinced now that I can accomplish anything I try as long as I take my pills. He wants to retire part-time and travel around the world with Krista. I'm going to run the business while he's gone. He'll fix my mistakes between short trips till I learn everything. Eventually he'll turn the chain over to me."

Little Bunny in charge of the whole company? She managed to choke out, "Congratulations."

"You'll help me, Frenchy, won't you? See, Daddy had you train me for a reason."

"Not because I was his best manager?"

Bunny just smiled. Frenchy thought of Clove's warning that her boss always got more out of her than he paid her for.

"That too. I wouldn't be so scared with you helping me."

Frenchy dropped to the couch. Bunny was practically young enough to be a trophy wife. She was pretty and mostly easy to be with. She had a big paid-for apartment with a view and had just practically inherited the Apple Cart. Plus she cooked like a chef. They could get married in Connecticut.

Bunny sat next to her. It was the first time Frenchy had seen her get all coy. She gazed up from under her eyebrows. "Daddy suggested I'd need a vice president."

She felt her eyes open wide.

"It's okay, Frenchy. It's only when Daddy's away. I need someone to keep after the managers. Do surprise visits. Be there for inventory days. Will you help me?"

"Dom's never hired a woman for anything higher than store manager!"

"Yes, he has, Frenchy. He's hired me. He thinks we're two peas in a pod, kind of innocent, but honest, with a love for the business."

"Innocent? Me? I can't take this all in."

"I guess it's a lot to ask all of a sudden." Bunny got that lost look in her eyes again. Sweat glistened at her hairline. Her right hand was wringing her left wrist. "All I really want is for you to come look at the sunset with me now and then, but I could use your help."

This was everything she always wanted, but in such an unexpected package. Her thoughts cascaded. She'd have to call it off with Gloria. She and Clove would stay just friends. She wouldn't need that glimmer of hope with Mercedes. Would Bunny object to her seeing her old flames? Could she still visit her SAGE lesbians? She'd have to resign from the condo/co-op board. Would Bunny travel if she got a condo in Florida?

She wished she had a pill to stop her own panic. Sucking in a deep breath she leaned back, one arm slipping across the back of the couch, behind Bunny. Could anything feel better than sitting beside soft, warm, needy Bunny on her pretty goldenrod-colored furniture in her comfy new home, listening to her birds sing and laughing at her stories?

CLEAN SLATE

Lisabet Sarai

I didn't cry until the last session.

Luisa picked up on it right away. "Should I stop? Do you need more anesthetic?"

I shook my head, the weight of my shame crushing me into the table. Tears leaked out from under my lids, closed against the hot glare of the examination light. "No, never mind. Just keep going."

"We don't have to finish today, chica. You can come back next week."

"No, forget it. Go on. I want to get it over with." It wasn't the deep burn of the laser that brought those traitorous tears. I'd endured a lot worse pain.

"Are you sure?"

I blinked in the brightness of that artificial sun, sending the moisture flying. Luisa hovered over me, an uncharacteristic frown knitting her coffee-colored brow. "I'm okay. Really." I managed a weak grin. "Don't mind me. It's just nerves." She looked unconvinced. "Please, Luisa. I promised Richard I'd be done by today."

"Whatever you say, Ally."

She picked up her instrument and focused the glass cylinder on my shoulder where she'd been working before. I closed my eyes, breathing deeply as she had taught me. The heat sliced into my skin. I welcomed the pain as the punishment I deserved for losing control. Not that Luisa would condemn me. She understood.

At first, she'd been Ms. Sanchez and I'd been Ms. Wells. Now, after four months, two days a week, she was practically a member of my family. Hell, I trusted her a lot more than family. Not that she'd told me much about her life or questioned me about mine, but I'm sure she recognized the Gothic letters inscribed at the back of my neck, the designs on my knuckles and in the crook of my elbow. She was an expert. She didn't need to ask.

Those tats were long gone. For the last four weeks, Luisa had been working patiently at the image that sprawled across my right shoulder and breast. My devil woman.

I called her Lilith. She had huge tits with red-grape nipples and a glorious fat ass. Her skin was black velvet. Her pomegranate lips parted to show pointed teeth that gleamed with my natural paleness. Lilith lounged naked on my chest, luxuriant jet curls tumbling across my shoulder, the globe of her butt coinciding with the meager swell of my own tit. Lilith grasped a steel-blue sword in one hand and a hank of chain in the other. Nobody fucked with Lilith.

I remembered her birth, long hours staring at the grimy ceiling, listening to the hum of the freeway traffic above, trying not to flinch as the needle bit into my flesh. No anesthetic in that joint; I was lucky if they sterilized the needles. Not that I cared, back then. The Westwood clinic where Luisa worked was a different world. It had private rooms with spotless white walls and peach upholstery that matched the towels. One session here cost more than my old mates would see in six months—unless they pulled a job.

Richard was paying, of course. I scrunched up my eyes, forcing back the returning tears.

"Too much?" Luisa's cool hand settled on my brow. Her low, liquid voice flowed over me, soothing the hurt away. "Want a break?"

"No, no, keep on. Thanks." Luisa was probably no more than a year or two older than I was, but she had the nurturing spirit of someone far more mature. I wondered sometimes if she had kids. She would be a great mother. If it hadn't been for Luisa, this whole thing would have been even more difficult.

I was the only white girl in the gang. They let me in anyway, when they realized how angry I was and how much I could take without breaking. They saw what we had in common: my dad who hanged himself when his deals went sour, my mom who tried to drink herself to death, my brother who raped me. So what if it was in the front seat of a BMW?

They gave me my first tat when I was sixteen. I'd chosen Lilith myself a year later. She was the woman I wanted to be. Voluptuous and tough and mean as hell. A predator. Not some pale, fashionably skinny blonde with tiny tits, hazel eyes, and a perfect WASP nose.

Now Luisa was erasing her, dot by dot, using bullets of light to dissolve and scatter Lilith's bitchy beauty. Lilith didn't have a future. Neither did I, if I had insisted on keeping her.

"There. That should do it."

Luisa switched off the chrome-circled exam light. I shivered in the suddenly cooler air. She swabbed my shoulder with a soft wipe soaked in antiseptic. My skin still numb from the anesthetic gel, I felt as though she was touching me through a layer of plastic wrap.

The damp cloth slipped down over my breast, an area Luisa had finished more than a week ago. The contrast pulled sensation into sharp focus. Tingling electricity danced across my flesh, raising goose bumps on the tan circle around my nipple. The nipple itself stood at attention, twice its normal size.

Luisa swished her wipe across that peak. Lightning arced from there to my pussy. Wetness bloomed there but did not quench the fire she had kindled. I searched her lovely dark eyes. What was going on?

Tension crackled between us. I saw raw desire flicker across her face, shattering her usual calm. My body tightened, nipples in aching knots and pussy clenched like a fist. My heart slammed against my ribs. Adrenaline coursed through me. I wanted to grab her. I wanted to run.

Then the moment passed. Her mask slipped back into position. Her ripe lips curved into a polite, professional smile. "It's finished, Ally. Come see." She snapped off her gloves, grasped my hand, and pulled me to a sitting position.

No. I didn't want to look. For the last two months Richard and I had made love in the dark, at my insistence. I had dressed in the closet, away from the mirror. I didn't want to see the changes in my body, my past evaporating week by week, dot by dot.

"That's okay," I said, reaching for my blouse. "I'll wait until the redness fades."

"Don't be afraid," Luisa said, her voice suddenly soft. "It's perfect. I don't think there will be any scarring. Please, take a look."

I heard the pain behind her words, the barely suppressed pleading. How could I be so selfish? Clearly she took pride in her work. What a silly bitch I was being, robbing her of that satisfaction! I swallowed hard and allowed her to lead me to the full-length mirror. My eyes were screwed shut.

Luisa stood behind me. She did not release my hand. "Open your eyes, Ally," she whispered in my ear. "See how beautiful you are."

Blinding white, like a field of pure snow, my vacant skin gleamed in the tasteful recessed lighting. The skull that had winked at my navel was gone. My flat belly was a bleak expanse of unmarked flesh. The barbed wire bracelet circling my left bicep—souvenir of the half-year of time I'd done—gone too. Worst of all, there was no sign of Lilith. My blunt-cut blond hair grazed the pale shoulder where her curls had rioted. My paltry breast was no longer hidden behind her sassy butt cheeks. She had been stripped from me, leaving me bare, empty, and utterly alone. And I had let it happen.

"No!" I screamed. Terror shot through me. I wanted to run, but all I could do was stand there, my whole body trembling, gazing at my horrible nakedness.

"Shh," Luisa murmured. She slipped her arms around my waist and pulled me against her solid warmth. "I know...I know... It's like this sometimes. You'll get used to it."

"No..." I whimpered. I struggled for a moment, but it was futile. She held me tight. Defeated, I relaxed into her embrace. Her lab jacket was as white as my skin, but the cinnamon-brown hands resting on my stomach were a welcome contrast to my paleness. I leaned back into her strength. Her breath tickled my ear.

"You've got to let go, chica," she whispered, while her hands migrated upward to cup my tits. "You've got to move on."

I watched, fascinated, as my little breasts disappeared under her palms. Her thumbs flicked at the tips and it was like she'd thrown a switch. High voltage sizzled up my spine. She ran her tongue along the edge of my earlobe. I quivered under the gentle assault, my knees weak. Fight it, I told myself; hold on to the outrage. You're irrevocably damaged and it's her fault. But I wanted to surrender, to let her soothe the pain away, if only for a little while. And I knew in my soul that I couldn't blame her for anything. There was no one to blame but myself.

She captured my nipples and rolled them back and forth like dough. She was turning up the volume, turning on the tap. Moisture poured into my cunt. Richard wouldn't like this, came a fleeting thought. Then she pinched them, hard the way I've always enjoyed, and sensation smothered my concern.

"Luisa..." I moaned as she palmed my mound through my pink silk panties—yet another gift from Richard. She rested her hand on the soaked fabric, allowing the pressure to build. I squirmed in her grasp, but she held me fast while continuing to play with my nipple. Meanwhile her middle finger stroked back and forth along the line of my cleft, pressing the silk into the soft, wet depression. My inner muscles clenched and my clit throbbed, screaming for direct stimulation.

Again she seemed to read my thoughts. She snaked her hand under the elastic and sank two fingers into my hungry cunt. Her thumb grazed the swollen nub poking through my sparse pubic curls. A pre-orgasmic shudder shook my frame. I slumped in her arms, a quivering mass of nerves, while she worked my pussy, coaxing me ever closer to the edge.

"You're so wet, chica," she purred. I was. Her fingers slipped and slithered in my depths like eels in the ocean. "I'm wet too. I've dreamed about this, about you...since the first day you shed your clothing and showed me your marks, I've wanted to strip you bare and make you writhe..."

"Oh...oh...oh!" I was beyond words, though some distant corner of my mind still observed, commented, analyzed. As though impatient, she pushed the panties down around my thighs, then plunged her whole hand into my sopping pussy. I ground my clit against her knuckles and spread my legs as wide as I could. Elastic cut into my flesh, but I didn't care. I opened myself to her clever fingers, wanting more, more—more of the fierce heat she coaxed from my snow-pale body, more of the pleasure she woke everywhere she touched.

She nipped at my shoulder, where the anesthetic had started to wear off. Pain sliced through me, a startling contrast to the sweet heaviness pooled between my thighs. I turned my head and she fastened her ripe-plum lips on mine, forcing her tongue into my mouth, still twisting my nipple and stabbing at my clit. She smelled like orange blossoms. She tasted of espresso. She pressed her pelvis against my bare ass. The starched fabric of her lab coat rasped against my cheeks. I could feel her dampness, even through the layers of cloth. I felt her want, a mirror of my own.

Somehow we ended up on the tiled floor. Under her coat she wore tight jeans and a purple tank top without a bra. Cradling her full breasts in my pale fingers, I sucked first one taut nipple and then the other while she struggled with her pants. I ran my tongue up along the outside of one luscious mound, to the sensitive spot under her arm. She stiffened and moaned. I heard tearing fabric and understood that she was as desperate as I.

I straddled her, pressing my lightly furred bush against her black thicket. Skin on skin, at last! My juices mingled with hers as we rubbed together. Our rich, musky scent hung heavy in the sterile room. I leaned over to capture her mouth, letting my pea-sized nipples graze her more opulent ones.

She relaxed and let me take the lead. I wanted to devour her. I had to hold myself back. I kissed her ferociously, for a long time, until I could tell she was having trouble breathing.

"Want...to...taste you...chica," she gasped when I finally released her. I could only grunt. I was too deep into my lust to speak. I nipped at her earlobe, then swung around so that my cunt was in her face. She spread me wide with trembling fingers.

The first sweep of her strong, hot tongue gathered me and drew me to the pinnacle. The second stroke pushed me off. My body took flight, arrowing up into clouds of pure pleasure, then tumbling downward to burst against her face. Everything poured out of me, the darkness and the fear and the shame, flooding her eager mouth.

I twitched for a while while she lapped at me gently. Finally, the ocean scent rising from her pussy lured me back to consciousness. I buried my face in her folds, wanting to give her the same glorious release she had drawn from me. Her moisture coated my cheeks. I could feel my own juices dripping down my thighs as I worked my tongue into her and flicked at her clit. She had the salty tang of a margarita. I reached around to grab her buttocks and opened her like a ripe fig, then sucked out the juicy pulp.

I could feel the tension gathering in her, could taste the imminent storm. I sucked harder, probed deeper, forgetting everything but the slick, smooth flesh I was consuming. My whole world contracted to the rosy purse of her sweet cunt.

Suddenly she clutched at me, digging her nails into my thighs. Her clit swelled against my lips. With a wail, she came hard, jerking her hips, slamming her pelvis against my mouth. I drank up the wetness that spilled from her, then planted soft, wet kisses along the insides of her thighs as her lush body gradually relaxed.

I lay quiet for a while, my ear on her plump belly, listening to her heartbeat. Strange pride blossomed in my chest. I couldn't remember the last time I had felt so good.

The shriek of my mobile broke the spell. I clambered to my feet and rummaged in my pocket. I knew who it was before I looked at the display.

"Hello, Richard."

"Hi, hon. How's it going?"

"We just finished." Guilt stabbed me in the gut. Richard was not the jealous type, but I'd told him about the women in prison. I knew he wouldn't approve.

"Great! And this is the last session, right?"

"Right." My throat tightened. The old darkness closed in on me. I hoped that he wouldn't hear it in my voice.

"I can't wait to see you." My fiancé's enthusiasm was obvious. "Shall I come pick you up on my way home from work?"

"No, that's okay. The traffic would be murder." Panic made my pulse skitter. "I'll take a cab. I'll see you at the condo in an hour or so."

"Wonderful, hon. See you then. I love you."

I flipped the phone shut and began to get dressed. My body felt stiff as wood.

"You don't have to marry him, you know." Luisa sat cross-legged on the floor, looking comfortable and unquestionably gorgeous. My cheeks grew hot. With amazing grace, she rose to her feet.

"Of course I do."

"Do you love him?"

Luisa stood in front of me, strong hands on her ample hips. Her flawless skin gleamed with sweat. I could still taste her arousal on my lips. Her warm smile made me quiver inside. It struck me that, except for her shorter hair and lighter complexion, Luisa looked quite a bit like Lilith.

"Um...I think so. He saved my life. He's done so much for me..." Life without Richard? I couldn't conceive of it. He'd been my rock, my anchor, for more than a year, ever since the trial.

"Gratitude is not the same thing as love, Ally."

"But I owe him so much. Just think about how much he spent for this, for you..." I was blushing again, stammering, confused by Luisa's closeness, terrified by the gulf of possibility she had opened before me.

"You could pay him back. I'd help." She brushed a blond lock out of my eyes. I thought she was going to kiss me, but she held back. "It's up to you. You're free to choose. You can leave the past behind—your life is a clean slate now. You can be whoever you want. Have whomever you want—Richard, or me, or maybe someone else entirely. But don't make your decisions out of guilt or shame or a sense of obligation."

"I don't know..." I couldn't get my mind around what she was saying.

"Trust yourself. You're tough and smart. If you weren't, you wouldn't have survived. Ask yourself what you really want." Luisa had donned her lab coat over her nakedness. She handed me my clothes. "Don't you think you deserve some happiness?"

Did I? The notion was bewildering and exciting.

"I'll walk you out. Think about it, chica. What do you really want?"

She kissed me, long and hard, before she opened the door, and I thought that I knew. But she put a finger to my lips before I could speak.

"Spend some time considering your options. There's no hurry. If you want me, you know where to find me."

She seemed so confident, it was difficult not to believe her.

I slipped on the leather jacket Richard had bought for me and went out to hail a cab.

THE QUICKENING

Siobhan Colman

My mistress calls to me. On moonless nights when the wind howls at my casement and the candles on the mantel dance like devils, she calls.

It was not always so.

Three winters ago she was a living thing. Warm skin, pink in the firelight, lips red and wet from biting them. She would sit and read to me, there, by the hearth and I would catch the swell of her breast through the clean white cotton of her shift.

"What story will it be, Mary?" She would run her fingers along the books on her shelf. Such books! Covered in the finest leather. Full of places I could only dream of. For I had no learning, though I could write my own name. My mistress had taught me that much already. But I could not read, though she promised I would master my letters.

"'Twill take time, my Mary, but you are quick-witted and observant. Study your letters and you will read soon enough."

I wanted to study hard and please her. "Yes, miss." But I wanted to study *her* more than I wished to look upon my letters.

"Shall it be Romance?" she asked. "Or Mystery?"

I did not care, though I liked to hear her read. "Something long, miss. I do not mind which." I was laying out her clothes for the morrow.

"Romance, I think. Will you brush my hair as I tell it? I do so love how softly you brush."

"Of course, miss."

She was the first mistress I'd ever known to ask me to do things for her. All others bellowed orders without a kind word. My mistress was different from my first day of service. Perhaps it was because she was not much older than me, but I think it was because she was never harsh. Born as sweet as any lamb. She has brought out the sweetness in me. I always thought myself clumsy and awkward, but she said I am gentle and graceful. Perhaps I am mad, for I feel she has made me gentle. She has made me what I am in her company. My own better self.

I took joy from the feel of her hair between my fingers. Silk it was. Dark silken threads, finer than any I'd ever known and I'd bend my nose low to breathe in the smell of it. It smelled of chamomile and oranges and shone like molasses in the firelight. And she'd read from her book, leaning her head against my hands as I brushed beyond counting. But in truth I wanted to run my own fingers through her hair. Catch the tresses in my hands and bring my lips to them. Warm her sweet throat with the heat of my breath. How I longed to be her brush, and beyond that, I wished myself incarnate in her book, gazed upon and delighted in. For I knew from experience that a lowly maid is no more than a wall or a table to her mistress.

Though she did not make me feel that way.

One night as I brushed her hair she put her book upon her lap and turned to gaze at me.

"Mary," she said, taking the brush from my hand and catching my fingers in her own.

"Yes, miss." My face was aflame. I could feel it. I looked down at our fingers entwined, for I swear I felt her tighten her hold. And I felt a charge run through me, catching my breath before settling in my belly.

"Do you have a sweetheart?" she asked, her gaze shifting from our hands to my face.

I stared at her, her face earnest, expectant. I could not tell her that I did, indeed, have a sweetheart, and it was she. For it was not my place to love my mistress, though I did with an ache as sharp as any thorn.

"I do not have time for courting, miss. My duties are here."

She stared at me intently, her eyebrow raised. Did she notice that I did not answer her question? "Everyone must have someone to love, Mary." She put the book down upon the mantel and stood. Her hand still held my own. "And to love them."

I could not speak, for my heart was pounding. I shifted upon my feet to steady myself and quieten my heart. It was then she released her hand from mine and stepped forward. "Mary, you are quite flushed. Are you ill?" Her fingers touched my cheek and I could not help but reach up to catch her fingers and hold them there, cool against my flesh. Oh, the velvet of her skin upon my cheek! I closed my eyes to hold that moment, for I felt I must be dreaming. She gazed at me then, her eyes wide, her own face flushed.

"Here, let us sit you down," she said, though her voice was strange. I expected her to step aside and give me her chair, but instead she put her arm about my waist and led me to her bed.

"No, miss. I cannot sit there." I stared at the white coverlet and the rich embroidery which decorated it. *SW* was stitched in roses and violets at every corner. *SW.* Sarah Warren. I knew each flowery initial keenly as I did all things belonging to my mistress. But I had never dared myself to imagine that I would ever be permitted to sit, there, upon her bed.

"I insist on it!" She pushed me gently so that my knees buckled and I found myself sitting on that embroidered garden. Then she stood before me and studied me, smiling. "I'm willing to bet that you have found my question a trial. I did not mean it to be. I just wanted to know more about you." She touched my hair. "For you are so quiet, Mary." She dropped her hand to her side. "I'm afraid you are unhappy. And may choose to leave me."

I blinked at her. "Oh no, miss. I will never leave you," I said more passionately than I realised. "For you make me happier than I have ever been!"

It was she who blinked now, her cheeks flaming as I watched her. What had I done?

At that moment a coal from the fire shifted and tumbled onto the grate. It hissed and smoked and she turned now toward the sound. I was grateful for it.

"Perhaps it is too warm," she said. "I shall open a window." And she crossed to the far end of the room.

"Miss!" I rose from the bed. "You must let me do that."

"Don't be silly." She lifted the curtain and pushed open the casement. "It is no trouble." A cold gust of wind breathed against the fire, and another jagged piece of coal hissed and fell into the ash. "Heavens, Mary, 'tis a restless house tonight," and she turned from the window to look at me as I stood on the rug beside her bed. "Will you not sit again?"

"No, miss. I am recovered. The cool air has proved a tonic."

She frowned. "Please sit again, Mary. You may have the chair if you prefer."

I did not move, for I confess I did not know where to put myself. "I have not finished my duties, miss."

She did not stir from beside the window, though the wind was cold. "What duties are these?"

I looked across to the fire and the copper pan beside it. Each night I placed hot stones within the pan to rub warmth between her sheets and take the chill from my mistress's bed. I found myself blushing. "I have not yet warmed your bed, miss."

She smiled. "You would surely have warmed it had you remained in it."

I felt my heart beat like a soldier's drum.

"There are no more duties for you tonight, Mary," she said, her voice carrying the smile on her lips. "Except to tell me about yourself." She stepped toward the fire and dragged a stool from the corner beside the hearth. "Please sit." As I headed for the stool, she promptly sat on it and laughed. "No, Mary. Tonight you must have the chair."

Again I found myself unable to move. "I cannot, miss. It is not fitting." My cheeks burned. "Please, miss, I would have the stool if I must sit."

"I seek another perspective, Mary. I would have you do the same." She motioned to the chair. "Please."

So I sat upon her fine chair, my hands restless in my lap, my back stiff against the cushion.

"Tell me about yourself, Mary."

"What would you have me say, miss?"

"I am not asking for more than you have of me."

I looked at her then. "I do not understand."

Her eyes were laughing. "Now, Mary, you know everything about me. You know I am quite alone in this house except for yourself, Corruthers, and Cook. You must know I care not for the opinions of my peers, nor for their company, that my needs are simple. I barely go to town unless it is to go to Meeting or to buy a new dress. And I dare say I've not bought a new dress in a while, though I've a mind to go tomorrow." She leaned forward. "And I've a mind to take you with me."

I'd never been out with my mistress. I'd never been beyond the front gate since coming to work in this house. "Miss?"

"We shall both have new dresses, Mary. 'Tis time."

"Time, miss?"

"Time." She nodded. "Now, I insist that you tell me about yourself. Your family, is it large?"

I thought about Ma and my brother and sisters. "Not so very, miss. I have four sisters and one brother. We lost John and Susie three year ago."

"There were eight children?"

I nodded.

She looked at me intently. "How did your brother and sister die?"

I pictured their tiny faces, grey upon their pillows, the exhausted sobs of Ma as she lay her wet cheek upon Susie's forehead. "'Twas the fever stole the life from them."

"Scarlet fever?" Her voice was gentle, almost a whisper. "Together?" I nodded again. "Oh, your poor mother!" and then, catching the look in my eye, "and yourself! 'Twas hard to lose them. I can see it. I am so sorry for you, Mary!" She took my hand. "How old were you?"

"Nearly fifteen years, miss. It was just afore I went into service."

"And your other brother and sisters?"

"Mostly younger than me. Except for Tom."

"Your father?"

I dropped my gaze to the floor, embarrassed. "He left us, miss. Found another woman. Tom took up men's chores early."

She blushed. "Oh." Then she smiled and squeezed my hand. "'Tis a good thing you have Tom. I'm sure your mother must be a fine one to have such a son." And then she stretched her fingers to touch my cheek so I would look up at her. "And *daughter.*"

My face burned. The place where her fingers touched my cheek was white heat itself.

"Is that why you came into service? To help your mother?"

I nodded. "'Tis easier on her to have less to feed, though I was fretful at leaving her. But in the years since she has been able to manage with Tom's money and the little I send her." I thought of Ma sewing by the firelight after the babies were in their beds. "Though I wish it could be more."

My mistress sat then and looked at me, her eyes searching my own so deeply I felt a pulling within myself that I thought must be my soul. I cannot say aught but that I *wanted* her to look at me, wanted to stay still with her eyes upon me and her face flushed with looking. For she gazed at me like she'd never looked at any book. And the knowledge sent the blood through me though I thought at the same time I might indeed die under her watch. For my heart now hammered in my chest.

"Would you stay with me this night, Mary?" Her voice was soft, hesitant.

"Of course, miss. I will keep watch." The wind was howling through the window and I thought she must be afraid, though my mistress had never been afraid before. "I will stoke up the fire for you too, miss. Bring up more coal."

She shook her head. "I don't want you to keep yourself awake. Not for me. I said your duties are finished, Mary." She reached out to take my hand. "I want you to stay with me, not as my servant."

"Not your servant, miss?"

"No," and she brought my hand slowly to her lips so that her breath was warm on my fingers. I was trembling. "Tonight you are not my servant." Her lips brushed ever so lightly across my fingertips. "I am yours."

I could feel my heart beating so wildly I feared I would faint, but as she brought her soft, pink mouth to my hand, I suddenly felt the shame of fingers smelling of coal and the vinegar from cleaning. In horror I drew my hand away. "No, miss!"

She seemed startled for a moment and then her face burned. She dropped her gaze to the floor as though she'd been scolded.

I ached to see her shamed when it was my own shame which ruined her kindness. "My hands, miss." I struggled to explain. "I am afraid they are so dirty you would think ill of me." I held them out to her. "The coal, you see, has made a home in them." I pointed to my fingernails. "Your hands, miss. They are so pink and clean. Like an angel's." I knew colour had risen in my own cheeks. "I'm sorry, miss."

She reached for my hand. "It is I who should be sorry. I did not mean to make you feel uncomfortable. But, Mary, you must know now that I could not think ill of you. There is nothing about you I find distasteful." Her eyes darkened. "In fact, I must confess I am drawn to you. And tonight, Mary, I do not want you to leave me, for I feel, suddenly, as though I have come to understand myself."

I could only blink at her words, but as she took my hand I found my fingers entwining with hers.

"Mary, may I wash your hands so that you've no need to fear that I will think anything but of the goodness in you?"

I nodded; though I knew it must be wrong of me to make a servant of my mistress, I did not want her to let go of my hands. She led me to her washstand and poured water in the bowl. Gathering the soap, she lathered her own hands, then wrapped them around mine, sliding her fingers across my palm and drawing circles across the top of my hand, teasing my fingers with her own, soft and soap-scented. And all the while she stood beside me, the warmth of her body making my own begin to burn, the sweetness of her breath as she ran her hands along mine, made me swoon with the need to wrap her tightly in my arms and taste her lips. But I could not.

And then her hands stilled and she took her jug and rinsed both our hands. I expected her to reach for her towel but instead she took my hands in hers and brought them to her lips. "Now they are roses," she whispered, "to match their owner." She inhaled and rubbed my fingers against her cheek before bringing them back to her lips. And then she did something which set my blood on fire. She kissed my fingers; then, opening her mouth, she took them inside.

I gasped. No sooner had my fingers discovered the warmth of her mouth than my own mouth sought the very place where they had been.

I cannot describe the sweetness of her kiss, nor the ache it awoke within my body. For I needed to feel the crush of her lips against mine. I needed to seek and hold her darting tongue, push my own tongue deep inside her mouth. She was not startled by my response. Indeed, she responded in kind until the press of our bodies sent her water jug crashing to the floor.

"Miss!" I pulled away. "The jug!"

She groaned and reached her fingers behind my head to pull my lips to hers. "Leave it," she whispered as her mouth found mine. Then she drew me into an embrace which left me trembling, for I could feel the swell of her breast against my own.

"Lie with me, Mary," she said, her body beginning to tremble. "I fear my legs are jelly."

I let her lead me to the bed.

"Here, let me." She knelt on the floor before me and unfastened my boots.

"No, miss!" I reached to stop her, but she caught my hand.

"Tonight I am your servant." She kissed my palm. The touch of her lips to that place made my heart pound. "I am Sarah. No longer your mistress." And she kissed the tender spot a second time. "Nor will I ever be again."

Slowly she loosened each lace and drew the boots from my feet, kissing my stockinged toes until I laughed.

"That's better." She stood and pushed me gently onto her bed. She was already in her nightdress and I felt her breasts upon my blouse as her knees parted my legs. She ran her hand along the wool of my skirt. "This won't do. May I free you of it?" I nodded and felt her fingers pulling at my buttons. In a moment I wore only my undergarments and blouse. "This too," she whispered, deftly undoing each hook and eye. "I want to touch you, Mary. If you'll let me."

Again I nodded, and my body became a bonfire under her fingers. My hands sought out her skin until the ribbons on her nightgown were loose upon the bed and my fingers held the warm swelling of her breasts, my thumbs dancing upon their darkened tips. Oh, how she groaned then, and arched her body upon my own! "Mary," she cried softly. "Oh, Mary," she cried again and pushed herself hard against me until I felt a pulse between my legs.

"May I taste you?" she brought her lips to my ear and whispered. "Here." She placed her fingers down to where the pulsing had begun. I did not need to answer. My body rose to meet her hand and she cooed in my ear as her fingers pressed against the spot. "How rushed your breath is," she whispered. "How warm and wet you are!"

Her fingers dipped, pushed, and moved against me, and I cried out from the pleasure of it. Then I sought her mouth with mine and felt her tongue move as her fingers moved and I had to pull my head away for breath.

"My dearest heart," she moaned, then moved so that her breasts lay firm upon my legs and her chin rested on my thigh. "I bet you taste of honey." And then her mouth was upon me and her tongue became a thousand darting fish.

There came a quickening then, so powerful and new to me that I cried out like a child born fresh into the world. And she held me, trembling as I trembled, her eyes wide and startled as I knew my own must be. And she covered me with kisses, saying my name as though it was a prayer and I told her I loved her, for I knew from that moment I was her sweetheart and she was mine.

Now, when the wind howls at my casement and the candles on the mantel dance like devils, my heart quickens and I wait.

HOUSE OF
MEMORIES

D. Jackson Leigh

I teeter down the steps and somehow manage to shove the huge box into the moving van. What the hell did she have in that box? Rocks?

"I've got to hurry or I'll miss the cable guy," she says, planting a quick kiss on my sweaty cheek. The kiss is clearly a ploy to distract me from the fact that the only thing she is carrying out of the house is her purse and two shoe boxes. "Can you walk through one more time to make sure we didn't leave anything?"

"Just make sure he gives us all the sports channels," I yell. You can't trust cable guys. The minute they leave, you usually discover they forgot to do this or that and it takes weeks to get them to return and fix it. But she's already pulling out of the drive. I sigh and turn back to the house.

The cabinets and closets are empty. The walls are completely bare. My footsteps thud hollowly on the hardwood flooring of the living room. But as I move from room to room, I realize the house is still full...cluttered with the memories we have made here.

The hallway reminds me of the first morning I woke in her bed. It was winter and cold. She slid from our warm cocoon and threw on a T-shirt. Just a T-shirt. I watched her hurry down that hall to adjust the heater's thermostat and nearly drooled on my pillow at the sight of her pale bottom dancing below the shirt's hem.

I realized I was heavily in lust with her.

The T-shirt was more erotic than the black teddy she'd been wearing when I had arrived the night before. I thought that little trip down the hallway was the sexiest thing I'd ever see.

Until the study.

We'd been dating for several months, and my weekends at her house were becoming a routine. I woke on Saturday morning alone in bed with the smell of coffee beckoning. I shuffled down the hall, smiling at a sudden flash of the T-shirt memory, then stopped dead in my tracks.

Hunched over the keyboard of her computer, she was wrapped in a short silk robe, her sleep-mussed hair sticking up in ten different directions and a pair of reading glasses perched on the end of her nose. It was adorable.

And I realized I'd fallen in love. It was another month before I confessed it to her.

That memory was made in the living room.

We had spent the evening lying in each other's arms on the sofa, kissing and talking and kissing while we pretended to watch a video of a Melissa Etheridge concert.

"I'm the only one," Melissa sang as our kissing evolved into slow, lazy lovemaking. She was still trembling from her orgasm as we lay heart to heart and I told her that I was the only one for her, and she for me.

As I shake myself from my thoughts, my last stop is the kitchen. I am careful to check the places likely to be overlooked, like the little cabinet over the refrigerator and the drawer under the oven. That's when I spot it. One of her favorite refrigerator magnets has fallen to the floor unnoticed. I turn it over and chuckle.

"If you can't take the heat, then get out of the kitchen," it reads.

Resting against the sink, I stare at the empty place where the dining table had been. I pocket the magnet and pull out one last memory, closing my eyes to relive it.

I have shed my shirt, walking through the house bare-chested to cool the flush of my arousal. I'm wearing my favorite baggy pair of soft faded Levi's because I need the extra room. While she has been scooping coffee, I have been making my own bedtime preparations. Did I say bedtime? With her, it can be anytime, anywhere. The thought of it makes my heart race and my nipples harden.

She is in her pajamas—soft blue to match her eyes—and busy over the sink, filling the coffeepot and setting the timer so we will awake to its warm aroma while we are still naked, wrapped around each other, legs entwined.

I approach her from behind and press my breasts to her soft shirt. She's taller and I have to rise up on my toes slightly to kiss the back of her neck. Her scent is warm and a bit tropical, like peaches warming on the branches of a Georgia orchard. I love her smell. It's clean and feminine like her.

I wrap my arms around her and hold her hard against me. I love the way my body feels against hers. I'm all muscle and she's so soft.

"I just wanted to get this coffee ready for the morning," she tells me.

"I just want to get you ready for tonight," I purr.

"Oh, yeah? Ready for what?" I feel the smile in her voice without having to see her face.

I turn out the lights and light a few candles around the dining room, and then check the back door locks.

"I want dessert," I tell her with a smile. I hold my hand out and beckon her over, pulling her into my embrace.

Sometimes I feel the need to be slow and gentle with her. I love her and want her to know the tenderness and respect I feel for her. Other times my need is raw and hot, and that's how I feel tonight.

I'm wet and tingle around the pliant double dildo that stretches me on one end and lies warming against my belly on the other. It took some concentrated relaxation methods and a handful of lube to prepare myself this way. Its girth between my legs, bulging my jeans, adds to my swagger.

She smiles at the rap of a deep-voiced singer I've put on continuous replay. It's the first song she played for me and she'd said, "It makes me think of you."

I dance against her, turning and rubbing my back against her breasts, my ass against her crotch. She loves my narrow hips and muscled butt, and I take advantage of that whenever possible.

"Remember the night of our first date?" My voice is low and husky. "We were so hot for each other, I thought I would throw you down on the dance floor and have you right there."

She plays along, dancing and smiling at my scene-setting.

"We could have gone into the restroom," she offers, alluding to another time when we christened the bar where we met with our ardor.

I dance around her and this time gyrate against her back, rubbing the bulge in my jeans against her buttocks and my rock-hard nipples against her shoulders. I am so very hot for her.

Coming full circle, I take her hands in mine, urging her back until her hips are against the dining room table.

When I push her to a reclining position, she protests. "I'm too heavy."

"No, you're not. Lie back and slide to the end," I command softly. I've always wanted to say that to a woman. Maybe one day I'll fulfill that gynecologist fantasy I have.

But this comes close. She lifts her hips as I tug her pajama bottoms and panties off, exposing her as I stand between her legs and draw her closer. The rapper is chanting about going crazy with love, and sex that is better than drugs.

I lick my way down her soft, white thighs and my mouth waters as her musk reaches my nostrils. I spread her open to my eyes and my tongue. My own juices trickle around the thick dildo as I feast on her wetness.

The power I feel in taking what is mine—what she willingly gives me—is fueled by her moans. I suck hard at her clit and run my tongue along the outside of her opening. I feel her grow hot and hard, and her breath quickens.

No, not yet, my sweet.

I take her to the edge, back off, then feast again while never allowing her release. Not yet.

I pull another, smaller dildo I'd left on an adjacent chair and lubricate it while I continue to lick. I tease her opening with it, pushing in a little, then withdrawing. She opens to me as I slide it in and out, keeping the rhythm in time with my tongue and the rapper's croon for his lady to "do what you do to me."

I feel her tense. She's too close.

Not yet, love. I'm only preparing her to be really filled.

I grab her hands and pull her to a sitting position. Smiling at the confusion I see in her eyes, I cover her mouth with my own before she can protest.

Our kiss deepens. She sucks my tongue and reaches for the zipper on my pants. She slips her hand inside, stopping for a moment when she feels my surprise. Her hand wraps around the cock and strokes so that it pushes deeper in me. I am swollen and hot where it rubs me.

"Turn around," I tell her. It is more of a request than a command. She complies and bends over the table as the rapper instructs "feet to shoulders, you know how we do it."

Her hips are soft in the candlelight. I love her ass. I kiss her smooth skin while spreading generous amounts of lube on the phallus that will connect my desire to hers.

I press in slowly, pulling out and pushing a little farther to allow her time to receive what I have to give. She grunts as I push in deeper and wait for her to adjust to its thickness.

I use my feet to push hers farther apart so I can lean over her back, brushing my nipples against her skin. Reaching around to tease her clit, I begin a slow thrust of my hips. I close my eyes and tremble against the urge to rush. Each stroke fills me as it fills her.

"Oh, baby," she moans.

I'm sliding in and out smoothly now, so I pick up my speed. She begins to whimper, and I signal my own impending orgasm with urgent grunts I know she will recognize. I shift for better position and thrust hard in a fast *slap, slap, slap* of my hips against her buttocks.

I can't hold out as a climax swarms up from my clit and explodes in my belly, but I keep pumping and stroking her clit until she screams so loud that I wonder if the neighbors are dialing 911.

She finally reaches behind to still my motion and I lie heavily on her to catch my breath, to slow my pounding heart.

"I love you," I whisper.

* * *

The ringing of my cell phone jerks me back to the present and I press my hand against the throbbing in my crotch as I answer.

"Where are you?" she asks. "I thought you'd be here thirty minutes ago."

"Is the cable guy there?"

"Here and gone. You won't miss a minute of the big game tonight."

"Do me a favor and set the DVR to record it. I'll be there in a bit. I'm going to stop by the grocery," I say thinking of the plump, ripe strawberries I saw there the day before. I hurry out the back door. "I've got other plans for us tonight."

I end the call and pull the door shut, realizing the memories are not in her house, but in my heart. Tonight, in *our* house, we will add to them.

A LOVE STORY

Evan Mora

T ell me a story."

A story, she says. "About what?"

"About us."

Of course. It's all a story, isn't it? All these hours and days, the big and the small, the changing of seasons. All these months, all these years. Her head on my lap, our fingers entwined, dappled sunlight filtering down through the canopy we're under, a solid trunk older than us all at my back.

"I once met this girl…" That's how it begins.

"Where?"

"In a town by the sea."

That's not where we met, but it doesn't matter to Kate. This story's about love, not history.

"Was it summer or winter?"

"Fall, I think; a gray, foggy day, on the beach. I was walking along—"

"Were you barefoot?"

"Of course. I was carrying my shoes in my hand. I'd been walking for miles, hadn't seen a soul, and then she was there, just ahead. She was throwing rocks out into the surf, and she was alone, like me."

It was winter, really, when Kate and I met, at the greengrocer, down in the village. She'd toppled a pile of grapefruit because, she'd later confess, she'd been looking at me. She's a bit clumsy, in an endearing kind of way, though it offends her butch sensibilities if I mention it.

"Did you speak to her?"

"I did."

"That was bold."

"I suppose. I told her she had a good arm. 'Thanks,' she said. 'I play shortstop for the Tigers, one of the summer league teams here in town.' I confessed I'd only arrived the day before. 'Here for Women's Week?' she asked. I said yes. 'That's too bad,' she continued."

"Why too bad?" Kate asks.

"I asked her the very same thing. 'It's not every day a pretty stranger happens by. How will I ever get to know you in a week?' she said."

"She was smooth."

"Very smooth," I agree with a smile, and I see Kate's chest swell just a little. It's one of the things I've always loved about her, the charisma that she's got in spades.

"Did she ask you out?"

"Not exactly. We just sort of wound up walking along the beach together. Walking and talking—and her voice—let me tell you, I could have listened to her voice forever."

There's no fiction in that, though Kate doesn't believe me. She always scoffs when I compliment her voice. *Nothing special,* she says. But she's wrong about that. Her voice is melodious and deep. It can soothe or excite, it's cultured and smooth, it can be fierce or tender by turn.

"What did you talk about?"

"I really don't know…trivial things, I suppose. It wasn't so much the things that were said, but the way that I felt that I remember."

"And how did you feel?"

"At ease, content. Talking with her seemed so natural. We were strangers, I know, but it didn't feel like we were. It felt like we were connected."

I tighten my grip on Kate's hand for emphasis, and she draws our laced fingers to her lips. She kisses my knuckles, soft lips, warm breath, and she nods that she understands. I brush a stray lock from her forehead and smile. My Kate, my hopeless romantic.

"I felt wistful too." I continue our story. "I felt such a pull to this woman, but my life was a thousand miles away, and hers was in that seaside town. When she asked me to dinner, I was ready to decline—"

"But why?" Kate interjects.

"Because I wasn't looking for a vacation romance, and I had a feeling she'd be easy to love…"

"So what happened?"

"She kissed me. Before I said no. Before I said anything at all. She kissed me, and I knew that wherever this path led, I'd follow it until the end."

It sounds crazy, I know, to say it like that, like it's *the big kiss* in some Hollywood romance. But while there might not have been any fireworks in the background, I remember the first time Kate kissed me just as vividly. The sweep of her tongue between my parted lips, the solid strength of her body pressed against me; the taste of her, like rich coffee and dark chocolate, and something altogether more life-sustaining.

"Some kiss." Kate smirks.

"Oh, indeed." I smile down into her eyes. "I'll have you know I'm a bit of a kiss connoisseur, and I'm not sure there's ever been another quite like it."

"Is that so?" She's fishing for compliments now, and I tweak her on the nose.

"The story?" I remind her.

"Oh right," she says. "She kissed you. So what happened then?"

"I accepted her invitation to dinner, of course."

"Of course. So where did she take you?"

"Her place."

"*What?*" Kate's indignant now. I've upset her sense of propriety. I can't help but tease her sometimes, she's so cute when she's all butch and irate. "She didn't even take you on a proper date? I don't care how well she kisses—"

"She was a chef, silly." I interrupt her mid-sentence. "She took me to her *restaurant*."

"Ohh..." Kate relaxes back into my lap, content to let me continue. "I always wanted to be a chef."

In truth, she's a corporate accountant. Boardrooms and bottom lines dominate her days, but she always dreams of something more exciting.

"It was Monday," I continue, "so the restaurant was closed. We had the place all to ourselves."

"Sounds romantic."

"It was—soft lighting, slow jazz, and a fantastic cabernet. I loved watching her work, she was so fluid and at ease, and let me tell you, the woman could cook. We ate and we talked, finished off the wine, and the hours passed by far too fast. 'I should go...' I sighed. 'But you can't,' she said. 'Can't you hear it? They're playing our song.'"

"What was it?" Kate asks, but she already knows, because this part? It's always the same.

"Louis Armstrong," I say and Kate smiles like she does. This is always her favorite part. I trace the lines around her eyes and the grooves at her mouth, evidence of the happiness we've shared.

"'A Kiss to Build a Dream On,'" I say, and Kate captures my hand, kissing the pads of my fingers.

"Tell me more." She's still holding my hand, and I pick up where the story left off.

"We danced, right there, in the middle of the restaurant, and it was like everything—"

"Just disappeared."

I sigh, just a little, remembering our date—the first time Kate and I had gone to dinner. A sleepy little French place in the East End. We'd talked until there was no one there but us. As the waiters swept up and set the tables for the morning brunch, Louis was singing in the background.

Dance with me? Kate had said with a smile. How could I resist? She'd kissed me, somewhere in the middle of that dance, and the world had just faded away. We'd kissed until the maitre d' had cleared his throat, politely telling us the restaurant had closed.

"So we danced," I say, getting back to my tale, "or we swayed, at least, to the music. And as clichéd as it sounds, she felt so right. It was like her arms were made to hold me."

"And did you kiss?" Kate asks.

"Oh yes, we kissed. But that was as far as it went."

"But you saw her again?"

"The very next day...and the next, and the one after that. We spent every moment that we could together, when she wasn't busy with things at the restaurant. She showed me her world and the things that she loved, and somehow she slipped into my heart."

That's the way it had been with Kate. We'd both fallen fast and hard. Kate had called me the morning after our date and asked me to dinner that same night. She'd said she didn't believe in playing any kind of games. *Neither do I*, I'd said. We'd been virtually inseparable from that day forward. We were married a year later, to the day.

"Before I knew it," I continue, "the week had passed, and there was only one night that remained. She asked if she could make me dinner again, but this time, in her home."

I pause to see if Kate will react, but she's quiet, so I go on.

"The meal was fantastic, if a little subdued. I think we were both all too aware this was the end. 'Should I put on a fire?' she asked when the meal was done, but I was restless, so I shook my head.

"'Can we see the ocean from here?' I knew it was close. We'd only walked a couple of blocks from the shore. 'Come on,' she said, grabbing wine and a blanket, and leading me up two flights of stairs. She turned in to a room that was clearly her bedroom, and I paused in the open doorway. 'Trust me.' She smiled, crossing to the other side and pulling open her balcony doors.

"It was beautiful, Kate, with the moonlight spilling in, and she beckoned for me to come outside. We sat side by side, wrapped up in her blanket, looking out at the reflection of the moon."

"I've always loved the ocean..." Kate sighs and I smile, thinking that in some other life she must have been a pirate, or a sailor maybe; she has such an affinity for the sea.

"We sat there," I say, "for what seemed like forever, listening to the sounds of the night, and somewhere in the middle of that, she whispered to me that she loved me."

"What did you say?" Kate asks quietly.

"Nothing. I started to cry. 'Hey now,' she said softly, cupping my face in her hands, 'that's not exactly the response I was hoping for.' 'I know,' I sniffed, 'I just can't believe I've got to go home in the morning.' It seemed too cruel a thing, to finally find love, and then to lose it before it had been realized. 'Do you love me?' she asked. 'What difference does it make?' 'All the difference in the world,' she said. I nodded. 'Yes, I love you,' and she kissed me before I could say more. We stayed like that, wrapped up in our blanket on her balcony by the light of the moon, kissing and touching, trying on this word 'love,' tasting it on each other's tongues."

"This story had better have a happy ending," Kate says, and her voice is a little gruff. It never fails to amaze me what a softie she is, despite her sometimes tough exterior.

"Are you going to let me finish telling it?" I tease, flashing her a little smile.

"Well, I'm just concerned—"

"You're concerned?"

"Well, yes. So you were in love, but didn't you still have to leave in the morning?"

"If you'd stop interrupting, I'd get to that part."

Kate harrumphs, but is quiet once more, so I pick up where the story left off.

"'I wish I could stay,' I whispered. 'You know,' she said, 'Chicago's a big city. I hear they always need more good restaurants.' I sat back, disbelieving—she couldn't be serious, and yet there was no laughter in her eyes. 'You couldn't—' 'Couldn't I?' she challenged. 'I've been restless here for a while. I've got a good manager; he can handle the place. Maybe now's the perfect time to expand. A little East Coast cooking in the Windy City…that is, if you wouldn't mind the company?' I started crying all over again and threw my arms around her neck. 'Yes!' I said, kissing her cheek, her lips, anywhere I could reach. She caught my lips for a deeper kiss, one that left both of us breathless.

"'Stay with me?' she whispered against my lips, and I nodded my assent. We went back inside, closed the balcony doors, and loved each other until morning."

"Happily ever after?" Kate says.

"Yeah." I smile. "Something like that. Being with her, it was everything. It felt like there had never been a time without her, and that everything we would ever do in our infinite future together was happening at that moment as well."

"That's how you felt about her?"

"No," I say. "That's how I feel about you." Kate kisses me then, the best feeling in the world, and one that no story can describe.

The sun's riding low in the summer sky, and that's always our cue to end. We pack up our blanket and head indoors. We'll make dinner, maybe watch some TV. And tomorrow or the next day, we'll do it all again, under the big beautiful tree in our yard.

"Next time," Kate says, "I want to be a pilot…"

ABOUT THE AUTHORS

CHEYENNE BLUE's (www.cheyenneblue.com) erotica has appeared in over sixty anthologies including *Best Women's Erotica, Mammoth Best New Erotica, Best Lesbian Erotica, Best Lesbian Romance, Girl Crazy, Girl Crush*, and *Lesbian Lust*. She thinks rules are made to be broken.

RACHEL KRAMER BUSSEL (www.rachelkramerbussel.com) is a New York–based author, editor, and blogger. Her anthologies include *Fast Girls, Orgasmic, Gotta Have It, Passion, Bottoms Up, Spanked, Crossdressing, The Mile High Club*, and others. She is senior editor at *Penthouse Variations* and writes a sex column for SexisMagazine.com.

SIOBHAN COLMAN's (www.siobhancolman.com) work has appeared in literary journals, anthologies and erotic magazines. Her stories "Sweet Treats at the CWA" and "The Emancipation of Elanora Pickle" have won the Mardi Gras Short Story Competition.

SHEREE L. GREER has been published in the *Story Week Reader*, *Hair Trigger*, the *Windy City Times*, *Reservoir*, and *Fictionary Magazine*. She is a recipient of a Union League of Chicago Civic and Arts Foundation Award.

THEDA HUDSON's work has appeared in *Best Lesbian Erotica 2011*, *Best Lesbian Romance 2011*, Renaissance E Books, and *Best S/M III*.

GENEVA KING (www.genevaking.com) has stories appearing in over a dozen anthologies including: *Best Women's Erotica 2006*, *Ultimate Lesbian Erotica 2009*, *Ultimate Undies*, *Caramel Flava*, *Peep Show*, and *Travelrotica for Lesbians 1 & 2*.

D. JACKSON LEIGH (www.djacksonleigh.com) has written three romances for Bold Strokes Books: *Bareback*, *Long Shot*, and *Call Me Softly*.

LEE LYNCH has written *Beggar of Love* and *Sweet Creek* for Bold Strokes Books and many others, including *The Swashbuckler*. She writes a syndicated column, "The Amazon Trail." Lynch is the recipient of the GCLS Trailblazer Award, an Alice B. Readers' Award, and the James Duggins Mid-Career Author Award.

ANNA MEADOWS is a part-time executive assistant, part-time lesbian housewife. Her work appears in *Best Lesbian Romance 2010* and *2011*, and *Girls Who Bite*.

JL MERROW (www.jlmerrow.com) has published over thirty short stories and novellas and is currently plotting murder and mayhem on the Isle of Wight for the purposes of her second novel.

EVAN MORA's stories of love, lust and other demons have appeared in places like *Best Lesbian Erotica '09*, *Best Lesbian Romance '09* and *'10*, *Where the Girls Are*, *Girl Crush*, *Gotta Have It: 69 Stories of Sudden Sex*, *Lesbian Cops*, and *Red Velvet and Absinthe: Paranormal Erotic Romance*.

CATHERINE PAULSSEN works by day as a freelancer; at night, she writes erotica.

Eroticist **GISELLE RENARDE** (www.wix.com/gisellerenarde/erotica) is a queer Canadian contributor to dozens of short story anthologies, an avid volunteer, and author of numerous electronic and print books.

LISABET SARAI (www.lisabetsarai.com) has published six erotic novels, two short story collections, and dozens of individual tales. She also edits the single-author charity series "Coming Together Presents" and reviews erotica for Erotica Readers and Writers Association and Erotica Revealed.

ANGELA VITALE is an artist in the Pacific Northwest. Her work has appeared on *Clean Sheets*.

ANNA WATSON is an old-school femme who married the butch of her dreams in the summer of 2010. She has selections in *Sometimes She Lets Me*, *Femmethology v.I*, *Girl Crazy*, and *Take Me There*.

ABOUT
THE EDITOR

RADCLYFFE has written over thirty-five romance and romantic intrigue novels, dozens of short stories, and, as L.L. Raand, a paranormal romance series, The Midnight Hunters.

She is an eight-time Lambda Literary Award finalist in romance, mystery, and erotica—winning in both romance and erotica. A member of the Saints and Sinners Literary Hall of Fame, she is also a 2010 RWA/FF&P Prism Award Winner, an Independent Publisher's award winner (IPPY), an Alice B. Readers' Award winner, and a 2011 finalist for the Benjamin Franklin, ForeWord Review Book of the Year, and the RWA Passionate Plume awards.

More of the Best Lesbian Romance

Best Lesbian Romance 2011
Edited by Radclyffe

"*Best Lesbian Romance* series editor Radclyffe has assembled a respectable crop of 17 authors for this year's offering. The stories are diverse in tone, style and subject, each containing a satisfying, surprising twist."—*Curve*
ISBN 978-1-57344-427-9 $14.95

Best Lesbian Romance 2010
Edited by Radclyffe

Ranging from the short and ever-so-sweet to the recklessly passionate, *Best Lesbian Romance 2010* is essential reading for anyone who favors the highly imaginative, the deeply sensual, and the very loving.
ISBN 978-1-57344-376-0 $14.95

Best Lesbian Romance 2009
Edited by Radclyffe

Scale the heights of emotion and the depths of desire with this collection of the very best lesbian romance writing of the year.
ISBN 978-1-57344-333-3 $14.95

Best Erotica Series

"Gets racier every year."—*San Francisco Bay Guardian*

Best of Best Women's Erotica 2
Edited by Violet Blue
ISBN 978-1-57344-379-1 $15.95

Best Women's Erotica 2011
Edited by Violet Blue
ISBN 978-1-57344-423-1 $15.95

Best Women's Erotica 2010
Edited by Violet Blue
ISBN 978-1-57344-373-9 $15.95

Best Women's Erotica 2009
Edited by Violet Blue
ISBN 978-1-57344-338-8 $15.95

Best Fetish Erotica
Edited by Cara Bruce
ISBN 978-1-57344-355-5 $15.95

Best of Best Lesbian Erotica 2
Edited by Tristan Taormino
ISBN 978-1-57344-212-1 $17.95

Best Lesbian Erotica 2011
Edited by Kathleen Warnock. Selected and
introduced by Lea DeLaria.
ISBN 978-1-57344-425-5 $15.95

Best Lesbian Erotica 2010
Edited by Kathleen Warnock. Selected and
introduced by BETTY.
ISBN 978-1-57344-375-3 $15.95

Best Gay Erotica 2011
Edited by Richard Labonté. Selected and
introduced by Kevin Killian.
ISBN 978-1-57344-424-8 $15.95

Best Gay Erotica 2010
Edited by Richard Labonté. Selected and
introduced by Blair Mastbaum.
ISBN 978-1-57344-374-6 $15.95

Best Gay Erotica 2009
Edited by Richard Labonté. Selected and
introduced by James Lear.
ISBN 978-1-57344-334-0 $15.95

In Sleeping Beauty's Bed
Erotic Fairy Tales
By Mitzi Szereto
ISBN 978-1-57344-367-8 $16.95

Can't Help the Way That I Feel
*Sultry Stories of African American Love,
Lust and Fantasy*
Edited by Lori Bryant-Woolridge
ISBN 978-1-57344-386-9 $14.95

Making the Hook-Up
Edgy Sex with Soul
Edited by Cole Riley
ISBN 978-1-57344-3838 $14.95

More of the Best Lesbian Erotica

Sometimes She Lets Me
Best Butch/Femme Erotica
Edited by Tristan Taormino

Does the swagger of a confident butch make you swoon? Do your knees go weak when you see a femme straighten her stockings? In *Sometimes She Lets Me*, Tristan Taormino chooses her favorite butch/femme stories from the *Best Lesbian Erotica* series.
ISBN 978-1-57344-382-1 $14.95

Lesbian Lust
Erotic Stories
Edited by Sacchi Green

Lust: It's the engine that drives us wild on the way to getting us off, and lesbian lust is the heart, soul and red-hot core of this anthology.
ISBN 978-1-57344-403-3 $14.95

Girl Crush
Women's Erotic Fantasies
Edited by R. Gay

In the steamy stories of *Girl Crush*, women satisfy their curiosity about the erotic possibilities of their infatuations.
ISBN 978-1-57344-394-4 $14.95

Girl Crazy
Coming Out Erotica
Edited by Sacchi Green

These irresistible stories of first times of all kinds invite the reader to savor that delicious, dizzy feeling known as "girl crazy."
ISBN 978-1-57344-352-4 $14.95

Lesbian Cowboys
Erotic Adventures
Edited by Sacchi Green and Rakelle Valencia

With stories that are edgy as shiny spurs and tender as broken-in leather, fifteen first-rate writers share their take on an iconic fantasy.
ISBN 978-1-57344-361-6 $14.95

Ordering is easy! Call us toll free or fax us to place your MC/VISA order.
You can also mail the order form below with payment to:
Cleis Press, 2246 Sixth St., Berkeley, CA 94710.

ORDER FORM

QTY	TITLE	PRICE
————	—————————————————————————————————	————
————	—————————————————————————————————	————
————	—————————————————————————————————	————
————	—————————————————————————————————	————
————	—————————————————————————————————	————
————	—————————————————————————————————	————
————	—————————————————————————————————	————
————	—————————————————————————————————	————

SUBTOTAL	————
SHIPPING	————
SALES TAX	————
TOTAL	————

Add $3.95 postage/handling for the first book ordered and $1.00 for each additional book. Outside North America, please contact us for shipping rates. California residents add 8.75% sales tax. Payment in U.S. dollars only.

* Free book of equal or lesser value. Shipping and applicable sales tax extra.

Cleis Press • Phone: (800) 780-2279 • Fax: (510) 845-8001
orders@cleispress.com • www.cleispress.com
You'll find more great books on our website

Follow us on Twitter @cleispress • Friend/fan us on Facebook

3 1901 04937 6520